AN EVANS NOVEL OF THE WEST

DOUGLAS SAVAGE

CEDAR CITY RENDEZVOUS

M. EVANS AND COMPANY, INC.
NEW YORK

M. Evans and Company, Inc.
216 East 49th Street
New York, NY 10017

Library of Congress Cataloging-in-Publication Data

Savage, Douglas.
    Cedar City rendezvous / Douglas Savage. — 1st ed.
      p.   cm. — (An Evans novel of the West)
    ISBN 0-87131-762-1 : $18.95
    I. Title.   II. Series.
  PS3569.A8223C43   1994
  813'.54—dc20   94-31985
                                                                      CIP

Designed by Charles A. de Kay
Typeset by Classic Type, Inc., New York City
Manufactured in the United States of America

First Edition

10 9 8 7 6 5 4 3 2 1

For Larry Ray Hurtt,
Who taught me the meaning
Of the word Brother

"There in ancient time the giants were born,
a famous race, great in stature, skilled in war."

—Baruch 3:25

Chapter One

MOST FOLKS WOULD NOT TRIFLE with the Hart Brothers.
Such folks walked. Some folks did not know better.
They are planted—not so deep as to keep the cold of the
high country from their bones, but deep enough to keep
the wolves from their place of repose. That would do.

"Don't know, brother Jason. I just don't know,"
Luke said softly through his red beard, which ended at
the deep lines etched into the corners of his eyes.

"Luke, where else we got to go anyway? T'ain't
been any pickings worth spit on the Overland for a
month. Got to be doing something. Have to earn a living somehow." Jason, the oldest of the brothers—a
broad-shouldered man with a dark beard—spoke into
the black chamber of his handiron. The 1858, New
Army .44 revolver lay in pieces on the rough table.
With the little finger of his right hand, he pried black
powder fouling from the cylinder. He studied the red-
bearded face across the table.

"May be, Jason. But can we trust that sheriff?" Luke
asked.

"Never been known to lie from what I hear. For my
money, his word is as straight as his shooting eye . . . I
say we go. What you think, little brother?" The big

man looked from his red-bearded brother to the clean face of the thin man beside him. "What you say, Samuel?"

"I'm with you, Jason."

"Luke?" asked the oldest of the brothers.

"With you, I suppose." He smiled weakly.

"And you, Frank?" drawled the oldest to the youngest.

"Don't want to ride home alone," the tall brother replied into the bottom of his glass. The youngest of the Hart Brothers laid his empty glass atop the dirty table at Lu's Saloon at Fort Owens, two weeks ride along the Overland Trail west of South Pass.

Jason wiped the grease from the pieces of his hand-iron.

The four Hart Brothers rose together. They drew their knee-length trail dusters over their gun belts. Their hard hands pressed wide, sweat-faded hats down low over their foreheads.

They walked to the long bar of the old saloon. Behind the bar stood two barkeeps: one young and lean, the other round and grizzled. The brothers stepped around brass spittoons on the filthy floor.

"For me and the boys," said the oldest as he plunked down a gold piece atop the bar.

"You be going to the Cedar City Rendezvous?" asked the young man behind the bar. He spoke nervously to the four living legends.

"Seems so," Jason said dryly.

As the four broad backs retreated toward the swinging doorway, the fat man grinned behind the bar. He lifted his open palm to the young man at his side. The youth laid the gold piece into the fleshy hand.

"Told you they was going," the short man said.

"Thought such as them was too smart to fall for it, that's all," the younger man mumbled.

"Smart? They're shootists, ain't they? They carry their smarts in their bedrolls." The thick man filled the stale air between them with his laugh. Outside, the four brothers churned up the dust as they walked toward the horses sweating under the broiling sun.

Jason arrived at the hitching post first. He reached under his sun-cracked saddle to tighten the cinches. His three brothers did likewise, squinting against the sun.

"I know you boys!"

The thin, hot air carried the hard words to the standing horsemen.

"I know you! Turn easy like. And fill your hands!"

The three younger brothers froze. Each lowered his hand to his hip. Only Jason continued to grip the horn and cantle of his worn saddle.

Jason stood at the outside of the four brothers. He felt the challenge at his back, but he did not drop his hands. Slowly, he lowered his dripping brow toward the saddle. His forehead touched the hot leather. With his eyes closed against the leathery smell at his face, Jason appeared as a man either asleep on his feet or at prayer. He swayed with his animal's restless pawing.

Above the clamor of men and women fleeing from the dusty street, the determined stranger filled the air with his impatience. "Ain't gonna wait all day!"

Jason raised his face from the saddle. Very slowly, he turned to face the figure at his back. As he turned, he came around into blinding sunlight. In his mind, he gave the faceless stranger credit for taking care to place the sun at his back. The oldest brother squinted tightly toward the figure fifteen paces away in the center of the dirt street. The unknown man shimmered in rippling waves of heat percolating from the hot dust.

The man in the street stood with his long legs wide apart.

"Your move, mister," called the man with no face through clenched teeth. The sun glinted on his gun belt.

Jason shrugged his shoulders inside his light trail coat. He slowly pushed the duster aside, behind his handiron low on his hip. He lowered his right hand beside the old Remington.

"Why?" the brother demanded. His voice carried the weariness of a man who longed to go but had to stay.

"I know you boys," the stranger shouted. "Seen your posters here or there somewheres."

The three brothers watched pensively from beside their horses.

"I'm here to prove that I'm faster and better. . . . Make your move!"

The four brothers had heard the words in other towns scattered, one just like the next, across the plains.

"I wouldn't, boy," Jason sighed grimly. "Go home. Leave us be . . . and live."

"Now!"

Before the man with no face could blink, Jason's handiron was raised at arm's length. The barrel of the piece was rock steady. The knuckles clenching the walnut grip were white.

The stranger's eyes were wide. His mouth gaped. The relentless sun melted him as he looked down the revolver fifteen yards from his face. His shooting hand had not even twitched, so fast did Jason clear leather. Jason held his aim on the stranger's heart.

Without lowering his heavy piece, Jason stepped toward this stranger who had chosen his own time and his own place to die. The three younger brothers followed. Their irons remained holstered.

Jason stopped eyeball to eyeball with the doomed challenger. So close did the two men stand that their breath mingled in a humid cloud of cheap whiskey fumes.

Jason pushed the muzzle of his revolver into the stranger's flaring right nostril. The Remington's black front sight disappeared inside the stricken man's head. The tall man swooned from fright and pain. With his iron buried inside the trembling man's face, Jason spoke in a hoarse whisper.

"Go home. Become an old man there. And if your face darkens my trail again, I'll blow it away. Clean away."

Jason returned his Remington, slightly bloody, to his hip. With his brothers at his back, he walked to his horse before the stranger could hobble on jelly legs from the street to vaporize into the shadows of the wretched town.

The brothers mounted silently and walked their mounts slowly from the dusty town. None looked back as the wide street filled with gawking people. Jason took the lead and rode with his bearded chin touching the colorless duster across his chest. Being a shootist exhausted him. He had not feared the long silence of death for years. But he was gnawed by the dead weight of knowing that the next town would be no different. The reputation of the Hart Brothers rode well ahead of them. Like some telegram full of sad news, it waited for them at every clapboard crossroads, most no larger than a saloon, a bawdy house, a jail, and the courthouse square for after-church hangings.

Riding into the sun, the brothers vanished in waves of heat where the horizon rippled like surf against a brown shore.

They rode southeast all afternoon. The animals panted in the choking heat. They rested the horses every hour beside the deeply rutted dirt road. Through narrow ruts carved by thirty years of wagon wheels, scorpions danced between the ponies' hooves. The brothers took care to water and rest their mounts since they could not eat each other if their provisions ran out.

By day's end, the riders arrived at the headwaters of the Bear River, which winds southward along the Overland Trail toward its great lake a two-day ride south. One day's terrible ride to the east lay the Sublette Cutoff two days this side of South Pass. Here along the Bear's white water, they could rest and lay their wind-burned faces in the cool water.

By nightfall, a fire burned in a firepit dug into the sandy earth. Chill replaced the dry furnace of daytime. The four riders sat draped in their bedrolls. Across the darkened plains, a crisp wind blew from the west.

In the darkness, they silently sipped hot coffee. Words pale before the wild places of the earth. A lone wolf howled to the white moon, which cast short shadows upon the arid nightscape.

Each brother took the silent comfort of his memories where lonesome men dwell among the familiar smells of long gone hearths. In the solitary wild places, men learn to live among the well-worn furniture of their minds.

"I was home," the youngest brother said softly, opening his eyes beside the fire.

"Me too, Frank," smiled Luke.

"It's time we slept." Jason threw cold coffee hissing into the fire. "Tomorrow we ride south."

The four men pulled their blankets to the chins where they lay with their heads on their saddles. On the far side of the little fire, four horses stood quietly. Behind his eyelids, each resting man flew his steady course to his own place of friendly company, freedom from cold, and the sweet tastes of home.

Chapter Two

WITH ONE CONVULSIVE MOVEMENT, JASON reached for his handiron hidden beneath his saddle under his head.

When his fist grabbed only cold sand, he bolted to his feet. In the chilly air of dawn, Jason stood in his long woollies. He focused his blurry eyes in the morning gloom. His fingers twitched where his shooting iron should have been.

"Seemed a good precaution, young fellow," said the figure squatting beside the cold firepit. His right hand held the tin coffee pot, which had awakened the brother when the metal clanked against a rock.

Jason clasped his arms across his chest to keep warm after the snug bedroll. He kicked the nearest sleeping body; Luke rolled over and mumbled in his sleep. When Jason kicked him again, the big man rolled out of his blankets. He, too, reached in his sleep for his piece under his saddle pillow. He found only sand. Standing slowly in his long drawers, he shivered beside his brother.

"You boys do make a sight," the stranger smiled where he crouched at the cold embers. "Going to catch your death if you don't wrap a blanket about yourselves." He worked the firepit until a wisp of new smoke rose into the cold air.

The stranger's words woke the two other brothers. All four stood with empty hands.

"Didn't want you boys to wake up shooting before you opened your eyes. Your irons be yonder." He nodded toward the far side of their clearing. "Fetch 'em if you want, and your clothes."

Jason took the first steps. Kneeling to retrieve his revolver, he inspected the aged Remington's six ignition caps. The weapon was still loaded and primed. The three other brothers found their sidearms loaded and capped.

"Your business if you want to freeze," the new man shrugged toward the coffee pot warming atop the fresh fire.

Following Jason's lead, the brothers lowered their weapons and wrapped their blankets around their shoulders.

"Much better. Come sit by the fire. Coffee be steaming in a minute." In the first light of daybreak, the fire was sparking to life.

The stranger rose from his work. The new man towered above all of them, even over Frank—the youngest and tallest.

Standing with the fire between himself and the four brothers, the visitor's face caught the new daylight. The brothers took his measure silently.

The stranger stood well over six feet in height. He wore a black, knee-length coat and his spurs were silver above the sand. Behind him, the brothers could see their dozing horses still secured to their rope crosstie. Among them was a huge, dapple-gray mount whose saddled back was a full hand higher than his companions. His gray ears were laid back among unfamiliar company.

In morning twilight the brothers studied the stranger's black waistcoat; it did not carry a trace of the sandy trail. His black trousers were immaculate. The muscular figure stood under a fine black hat. The new sun played on his gold watch chain, which crossed his black vest and its brass buttons. Beneath the watch chain hung a heavy gun belt. Each side of the waistcoat bulged around a handiron. He crossed his long arms to keep them well away from his twin pieces.

"I am called the Deacon. Guess I know who you boys are." The square jaw smiled easily and confidently.

Before the brothers could force their words into the tense silence of the desert at dawn, steam wooshed from the coffee pot. The Deacon bent toward the fire and the five tin cups which he had laid beside the firepit.

"You're a sight, boys," he smiled, kneeling at the fire. The sun shone upon the brothers' long woollies, two sets white and two red. They were all union suits with a regulation trapdoor astern.

Luke shuffled through the cool sand toward his bedroll and his clothes—folded within the blankets to keep them warm. His two younger brothers followed. Only Jason lingered behind at the Deacon's side. He pulled his blanket tighter around his chilled shoulders. Not until his three brothers had dressed and had strapped on their gun belts did he retire to dress beside his saddle. The Deacon waited patiently with a hot tin cup in his hands until all four brothers came to the fireside.

In full morning daylight, the Deacon handed each of the brothers a cup of hot coffee. Each man offered a wary "Thanks, kindly."

The five men stood in uncomfortable silence beside the low fire where they sipped the bitter brew.

"Going south," the Deacon said softly. "What about you boys?" He squinted over his tin cup toward Jason.

"South, too," Jason said. He studied the Deacon carefully.

"The Rendezvous?" The Deacon's eyes narrowed as he lifted his tin cup.

Jason nodded without a word.

"Good," the Deacon smiled into his coffee.

Chapter Three

THE WILD GREEN MOUNTAINS OF IDAHO belonged to the Shoshone and the Arapaho Nations—destined soon to be dust under the white man's boots and wagons. Well to the north of where the brothers rode with the Deacon, the sun warmed the Bitterroot Mountains. There, the land ran with blood during the 100-day annihilation of the great Nez Perce Nation on the blades of General Oliver Howard and his Colonels Sam Sturgis, John Gibbon, and Nelson Miles.

In such hard country, white men kinned with the white men they could find. But white man or not, the four brothers had not turned their backs to the Deacon and his twin forty-fours. The big man carried centerfire Peacemakers, not the old cap and ball Remingtons and Starrs that the brothers carried.

Along the trail, the Deacon rode with two brothers on each side. From his horse's tall withers, the Deacon looked down on the riders at his elbows. They rode slowly eastward. After half a day, they walked their sweating mounts in the stifling heat of the highlands surrounded by green ridges. They moved away from the sun and no rider wasted energy on idle words. When the sun was high, they stopped to rest the horses in a little clearing off the trail within the cover of thin pines.

Each rider tied his animal's reins to a sapling. The winded horses lowered their faces to chew the scud grass while the men sat on fallen timbers. Six hours to the east lay Fort Smith, a grim outpost of pilgrims. The little fort held the promise of hot food and easy women.

"Best send the boy," the Deacon offered between drags on his canteen.

"Reckon so," Jason nodded. "Your face ain't made the posters yet, Frank. You should be able to pass safe enough if you can stay out of trouble . . . and just buy what you can fit in those saddle bags."

The youngest Hart smiled. "Only what I can carry."

The middle brothers said nothing. They let their weary minds wander to the things a body off the trail needed at Fort Smith worse than fresh powder or a real bed or jerked beef.

The Deacon rose in the dry heat. The brothers followed, tightening their animals' girths.

As the sun crossed the clear sky, the five riders walked their mounts eastward. They rested hourly to save the animals.

By dusk, Fort Smith lay only five miles beyond a little stand of trees beside the trail. The riders dismounted and took the cover of a deep ravine that fell away from the trail. After the Deacon and the three older brothers had brushed their animals with dry twigs, the men approached Frank who sat atop his tired horse in the twilight.

"Only what I can carry," smiled the mounted youth.

"Mind that," cautioned the eldest brother as he patted the neck of Frank's horse.

The tall youth pulled his wide hat down over his forehead and spurred his mount slowly forward out of the ravine.

"Ask about the doc," Samuel called toward Frank's back. The departing brother waved his free hand before resting it on the forty-four pounding against his side.

"And guard your hair," Jason called as Frank disappeared into the night. They camped in Shoshone country.

The Deacon and the remaining brothers dry-camped without a fire in the thick cover of the trees. The absence of a moon added to the utter darkness. Overhead, the brilliant stars did not twinkle in the thin and cold air of the high country. A shallow river ran through the lowest reaches of the ravine. The four campers wore their trail clothes inside their blankets to keep out the chill. Cold rations inspired little conversation.

"Reckon the boy is there by now," Luke said into the blanket pulled up to his beard.

AT MIDNIGHT, FRANK rode slowly through the main street of sleeping Fort Smith. A single lantern burned inside the sheriff's office. Frank had to pound on the closed door of the livery.

"How much for board and feed for the night?" the brother asked the irritated blacksmith who stood with a blanket wrapped around his long woollies.

"Two dollars gold," the liveryman snorted.

"Obliged," Frank nodded as he flipped two dollars into the man's large hand. The smithy led the sweating animal by his bridle. Frank followed.

"Put some miles on today, boy," the sleepy man mumbled.

"Some. What's open this time of night?"

"Just the saloon across from the courthouse." The blacksmith heaved the dusty saddle onto a wall peg as he shoved the warm animal into a stall. The tall horse promptly spread his hind quarters and poured a gallon of dark water onto the sand.

"He seems to like the accommodations," the youth smiled to the liveryman.

"Guess so. You can bed down in an empty stall, boy, if you have a mind. No extra charge this time of night." The smithy sounded friendlier although he did not turn toward the youth. The stocky man was already walking back to his own shack adjacent to the stable.

"Thanks!" Frank called into the night.

"T'ain't nothing."

The gold eagles lay heavily in the boy's pocket as he thought of the painted women and soft beds down the street at the saloon. He could hear their laughing voices over the steady munching of his horse two stalls over. The boy lay in his blankets atop a pile of clean, dry straw. Its warm, musty smell was faintly sweet and quite homey to the farmbred horseman. He smiled at the sound of heavy plops splatting on the earthen floor twenty paces away. Frank did not remember pulling his old hat across his face when sunlight poured in through the slits in the barn siding.

Fort Smith came alive under the purple sky peculiar to the high country. The morning air was cool on the weatherbeaten town.

Leaving the squalid livery, Frank rubbed the nose of his resting mount who was quietly content with fresh grain and clean water. He pulled his hat low over his brow to shield his eyes from the fierce sun. Wagon wheels already stirred the fine dust that hung in the dead air.

The youth entered the clapboard doorway of Lanza's Dry Goods and Barber Shop. Pleasant scents of spices, teas, and turpentine penetrated his nose long since numb from trail dust. He inhaled deeply and smiled toward the storekeep.

"Joe's the name, young fellow. What's your pleasure?" grinned a pleasant, white-haired merchant who climbed down a ladder from a wall of calico piled floor to ceiling.

"Need some trail stores," Frank nodded. He examined a glass jar full of hard candies.

"You'll not need to shop anywhere else, my friend," the older man smiled.

"Fine. Could use a sack of grain—something what won't sweat out. Oats, if you have it. Black powder, too. And roundballs in forty-four and Number Eleven caps. Oh, and maybe two plugs of your best chaw." He smiled, thinking of Luke who would be grateful.

The friendly man behind the counter eyed the lone rider's tattered clothes and his sweat-soaked shirt. Frank still had straw in his hair from his bed.

"Cost you, son."

The dusty customer laid a gold coin down on the counter between the jars of candy.

The storekeep raised an eyebrow. "Well, you appear to be well covered alright."

While the merchant fetched the order, Frank smiled and put his ratty hat on the counter. He picked up a fine Montana peak hat and fondled the hard, four-sided crown.

"That'll be another gold piece," the merchant called

from the back room as Frank admired himself in a wavy mirror.

Another gold coin spun on the counter. Frank blew a fleck of dust from his new hat.

"One more thing, please," the stranger with the new hat smiled. "My pa used to talk about old Doc Silverman. Thought maybe he settled out here. Maybe you know of him?"

"Doc Silverman?" the storekeep shook his head. "I've been here nearly forty years and the doc was gone before my time even. Why not stop over at the saloon at the far end of the street. The far end, mind you, not the fancy one this side of town. Just ask for Doc. He'll be there by now probably. He can tell you all about the doc you're looking for. And I'll have your stores all packed when you come back." The older man nodded kindly. "Say, where you heading anyway?"

"Me and my brothers are headed for Cedar City."

The merchant's face hardened. He frowned.

"At the end of the street, boy. Across from Pitcarin and Sons."

"Thanks," the youth grinned. He planted his new hat firmly atop his head.

The street was already bustling with morning traffic. The saloon at the end of the main street of Fort Smith was old and decrepit. The youth knew that this was the poor-man's watering hole and the place for drifters passing through from nowhere to nowhere.

"I'm looking for someone called Doc," Frank smiled to a sour-looking barkeep. Without looking up from a glass he was drying, the thick man nodded toward an old man whose face was hidden behind an uplifted glass. He sat alone at a small, battered table.

"Mind some company, old timer?"

The old man laid his empty glass aside. He glanced up with a worried expression darkening his leathery face.

"Do I owe you, stranger?" There was pain in the old man's red eyes.

"No, sir," smiled the tall man with the new hat. "Understand you knew Doc Silverman. My pa spoke of him often. Seems he doctored him long ago."

The old man stood up. To Frank's surprise, the sagging relic was taller than the youth. The old man was rather well muscled although his face was deeply lined.

"You're welcome to have a seat, boy, if you be buying."

The young man sat down and motioned for the barkeep who shuffled across the filthy floor.

"Two more," Frank called. "Tell me about the doc."

"I surely did know him. Many years ago. Did you say you knew the old doc?"

The old man looked anxiously after the barkeep who was in no hurry to bring the warm beers.

"No. My pa knew the doc. I'm just passing through. I thought I would look him up. For my pa."

Two warm beers were laid upon the knotty table. Froth formed a puddle between the glasses. The old man instantly raised a greasy glass.

"Passin' through, boy? To where?"

"Cedar City."

The old man paused. "Oh," he sighed. "Seen others goin' there."

Frank lifted his glass.

"What say you wanted with me, boy? Don't owe you, do I?"

"Pay as you go, old timer," the barkeep snarled through sweating lips.

"I got it," Frank said before the old man could speak.

"Obliged, boy." Doc folded his hands around the grimy glass. With a sigh, the old man closed his dry eyelids. The youth at his side wondered if the old man was napping in the middle of a sentence.

Chapter Four

"DOC SILVERMAN?" THE OLD MAN stammered without opening his eyes. "Sure, I know'd him. He first doctored me when I as no more than that high. No wonder, neither. Doc Silverman doctored near everyone in Fort Smith back when this place was nothing but a widening in the road.

"First time I seen Doc ride that big bay into town, I was standing in the alley beside the old courthouse. I was smoking. Pa—he would have broken my face if'n he saw me. You wouldn't recollect Pa.

"Well, old Doc rides in real easy like. Stops at the livery and carries his bag over his shoulder. Across his right one, like this. He walks across the dirt street and comes right for me. Burned my fingers dropping my weed into the dust. Scared stiff, I was. Thought he might know Pa! Why my bottom got hot just thinking about it.

"'Morning, boy,' says the doc. His face is covered with trail but he gives me this big, white smile. Real kindly, like he means it.

"So I smiled back at Doc. The sun is bright over his shoulder. Sun is shining into my face and I screw up my face 'cause of the sun. But I'm real careful to keep my boot on my cig, just in case.

"'Morning,' says I. I'm standing like this with my hand up to my face against that there sun, don't you see. 'You from here abouts?' says I.

"'No, son,' says the doc smiling that smile. 'Come in off the Overland from Fort Hall. Be looking for the town doc's place. You know it, boy?'

"Well, just then Doc he steps sideways, just enough so's the sun is square behind him. That's when I see that there scarf . . . wears it like some white necktie inside his coat. That white scarf atop his black vest makes Doc look like some old parson.

"'Doc?' says I. 'Doc got blowed away just t'other night at the saloon. Yes, sir. Doc got it right over yonder. Went to fetch some pilgrim what got plugged over a table. Doc bends over to listen to his chest with the hole in it. Doc uses his listening tube. When the other fella sees that there little tube for listening to folks' innards, he thinks Doc has a forty-four so he plugs old Doc, too. Just to be safe, I suppose.' Well, I give the new doc the whole story right there.

"'Where's the doc's office, boy?' he asks me. 'Up them stairs, over the dress shop,' says I. 'But we ain't got no doc now.'

"'Yes you do, boy. Much obliged,' says he. So he walks to the dress shop, right past where our old doc got it. He sort of waits a minute by the steps, by that old sign what reads 'Physician and Surgeon.' Think maybe he smiled at that sign. Then upstairs he went, right into the other doc's place. Yes, sir, I can still see that white scarf of his whipping in the wind.

"Never did see that big bay horse again. It was the fall of the year. What a grand time, that was! Guaranteed to have one shooting every Saturday night! Always shooting by them cow punchers in off the Goodnight-Loving Trail. And then some stranger gets carried stone dead over to Mr. Pitcarin's to get alkeeholled for to get planted. Old bone yard's still there.

"With every shooting, the new doc walks that long, slow walk of his to the saloon. He bends over the man with the new hole for a minute and Doc puts his ear right up to the pale man's chest. Then Doc gets up, shakes his head, and goes back to the stairs beside the dress shop. Sometimes, he gets blood on that white scarf what he wears every day, night or day. Doc says he pee-roxides the blood out of the scarf. He has all them little yeller bottles upstairs, you see. The medicine chest is beside the exam table, the one where the leather is worn clean through to the stuffings from all the folks what's laid there.

"No sir. The doc never rides that big bay no more. Folks mainly come to him. He medicines people upstairs and he gives 'em that smile, the one I told you about.

"When Doc Silverman gives you that smile and touches a body real gentle like, well they just up and gets well. Usually. When folks was birthing or when they was having a hard go up the flu, Doc would walk on over to their house. Let me go with him, he did. Doc would sit real still by the bed and I would carry the bag with them little yeller bottles 'n such as that. Doc he would just sit there however long the birthing or the dying took. When the dying was over, Doc would drop his chin like this and he would say something real quiet before going to the kinfolk. Me, I'm carrying the saddlebags full of little bottles. Walking home, Doc would knock on old Mr. Pitcarin's door. Never did wait for an answer. Somehow, Mr. Pitcarin, the undertaker, would just know where to fetch the new body for to get excavated.

"I recollect Miss Lois Ann. Most folks is gone who'd remember Miss Lois Ann. One time, Doc walks over to Miss Lois what got stoved up by her carriage horse. The Doc he sits by her for a long time. She's moaning something awful. Doc turns to me and he says, 'Wait outside, son.'

"That's when I seen it. Before I can get out of the bedroom, Doc is taking that white scarf off. Never done that before. I hear him moving around so I turns around to watch. That scarf is laid on the chair besides Miss Lois. Only one lamp is burning near the bed since it's midnight. Doc don't quite see me in the doorway. Up by his chin, where his collar ends—where that scarf always is—I see a fearsome scar. Goes like this all 'round his neck, thick and red and wrinkly like. Gives me the creeps. I mean all over I'm getting them little bumps standing on my neck. Never saw nothing like that scar 'cept maybe on someone laid out at old Mr. Pitcarin's and plugged into his little handpump. Had to take a rope off a body to see anything like what Doc's got going all 'round. When Doc sees me standing with my mouth open catching flies, he puts his hand up to his neck like this. 'Go on, boy', he shouts. And I'm gone! I waits downstairs for the doc.

"Doc finally comes down next morning at first light. His sleeves rolled up high. Has that scarf back where it belongs, too.

"'Well, Doc?' says I. Everyone loves Miss Lois Ann.

"'Just fine, son,' says Doc. 'Later today, you can come back to check on our patient.' Then Doc smiles and walks outside.

"'*Our* patient,' says Doc. Our patient! Right proud I was just then. Wanted to be a doc, too, awful bad. No taste for the smell later on, though.

"Well, it's me and Doc for a long time. Years, seems like. Pa says to me more than once. 'Boy, you spend more time with Doc than in the paddock. The livestock gonna starve to death.' But I don't pay no mind. After all, I'm going to be a doc, too. Just like Doc Silverman.

"It's spring one year when the whole town starts buzzing. 'The ranger's coming. The ranger's coming. Asking for Doc!'

"Well, you can imagine! I run up the street to the dress shop. Up I run to Doc's.

"'Doc! Doc!', I shout. 'Ranger's come looking for you!' I remember breathing powerful hard and the tears is falling down my face. I was still a boy. . . . But Doc is just asitting real calm at his old rolltop desk. He's got that scarf 'round his neck. Never did see him take it off, but that once. Doc is sitting with some big book open in his lap.

"'Ranger, you say?' says Doc. That's all he says, real easy like.

"'Yes,' says I. 'And he's packing a piece like a cannon!'" Well, I'm still bawling like a sissy. Doc looks the other way so's to pretend he don't see no tears. That was Doc for you.

"'Packing a handiron, is he?' Doc looks up and closes that big, black book. You could see a hardness come down over his face. Never seen that look before or since on Doc's face.

"'You got an iron?' says I to Doc.

"'You know I never pack, boy,' says Doc. 'Not any more,' he says real soft. He stands up and he's smiling.

But it ain't his reg'lar smile like when someone's birthing. Instead, it's a real hard little smile. Gives me the creeps, it does. Then, real quick like, Doc's hand comes up to that scarf 'round his throat. Up and down goes his hand, real fast.

"'The ranger will know where to find me,' Doc smiles to me. And just like that he sits down again and opens that big book. And he's reading! Ranger's coming and Doc is reading! It's like I just come on in to say that Miss Gertie's ankles is swoll'd and the mister wants to bring her up to Doc.

"'Run along home, son,' Doc says to me.

"So I go down them stairs into the street. And I walk right smack into the ranger. Like hitting a wall; I just bounce right off him.

"'Where's the fire, boy?' says the ranger. His voice is real deep. Like Pa's when he catches me smoking. Well I don't say nothing. I'm just standing there looking up at the man's handiron. It looked this big—but I was just a boy then.

"'Is the man calling himself the new doc up them steps?' says the ranger.

"I don't say nothing.

"'I imagine so,' he says. 'Move along, boy. Ain't you got school?'

"Well, I'm moving along alright . . . back up them stairs right after the ranger. The ranger is moving real slow up the steps. Like he's lamed up. He's favoring one leg like my pony when his front feet was sore and real hot to the touch. Pa says he were about to tan me good if'n it's founder. I did love that animal, more than any living body, 'cept Ma and Pa.

"The ranger went all the way up like that. Like he

has ringbone or something. He walks up like Miss Gertie when her mister is cussing a blue streak.

"Well, the ranger goes on into Doc's door. And I'm hiding in the dark stairway, real quite. I weren't hardly breathing so Doc can't hear me outside his door, listening. I'd take a breath, hold it long as I could, then let it out real slow. Like Pa taught me when we went into the mountains hunting. Pa taught me all a body needs to know about such as that. Funny. The older I get, the more I think about Pa. Starting to look like him by now, too. Wouldn't mind that.

"So I'm just standing quiet like death. 'Ranger,' says Doc. I can hear him. He's talking real soft with that voice what makes folks feel better just for hearing it.

"'Doc,' says that voice like slag going down a flume channel.

"'It's been a long time, Ranger. You come to finish your work with me?'

"'Not hardly, Doc. You know the law: only get one chance.'

"'Then state your business, Ranger.'

"'It's my leg, Doc. . . . Stopped a ball just below my knee.'

"Well, I'm still out on the stairs and holding my breath 'til I was about to die. Felt like one of Mr. Pitcarin's customers! Then I hear the exam table give a little creak.

"'Easy, Ranger. How's this feel? . . . What about this?'

"I hear the ranger moaning kind of quiet like and I can hear Doc washing his hands in the little china basin.

"'My God, Doc,' whispers the ranger.

"'Pretty work, isn't it, Ranger?'

"I'm really getting creepy now. I can imagine what Doc showed him when Doc takes off that scarf.

"'Lie still, Ranger,' says Doc. 'Take a few deep breaths of this. Smells like bad mash at first. Slow and easy, now.'

"'Don't carve too high, Doc,' the ranger says awful quiet.

"For a long time I don't hear nothing at all. Maybe for an hour. I only hear the door on the little medicine chest opening and closing a couple of times. I can hear them little yeller bottles jingling.

"Then I hear the ranger groaning a little, like a body sleeping off a bad drunk.

"'You're doing fine, Ranger,' says Doc after a while. 'Had to go down pretty deep to get the lead out of that leg. And your head will pound for a few days from the spirits of chloroform I used to knock you out. The leg should mend in a few days.'

"'Thanks, Doc,' says the ranger real weak like.

"'Sure,' says Doc. 'Just rest as long as you like there. I'll get you rooms across the street.'

"Then the ranger he says, 'Thanks. My head feels like a brass band in there.'

"'Yes,' says Doc real cold. 'Like the brass band you had for me at the courthouse steps?'

"The ranger he mumbles something I can't make out.

"'Forget it, Ranger. It was all a lifetime ago. Rest now.'

"I hear the Doc's chair creak when he sits down. I know that thick book is open for Doc to study. I start down them steps, quiet as a cat.

"'Doc? Should you look at this here leg again?' The ranger sounds real tired.

"'Ranger,' says Doc, 'I will only see that leg again at Pitcarin's.'

"That's all I hear up there. After a day or two, the ranger is limping about town and has rooms at the hotel. When I seen him with a chorus girl from the rich-man's saloon, I figure he's on the mend. And I seen Doc, too. As always, he's walking about town and smiling his feel-better smile with that scarf where it's supposed to be.

"By and by, the ranger left town all by his lonesome. Doc did not see him off, though. Doc and me was over to old Miss Gertie. She's going and the mister he's sobbing and spitting a blue streak. Miss Gertie is all gray, except where she's smiling up at Doc who's smiling down at her. I was standing in the corner holding them saddlebags with the little yeller bottles which was my place 'cause I was going to be a doc, too."

The old man seemed to nap while sitting slouched in his seat.

"Doc, boy? Oh, Doc stayed a lifetime. Him and his scarf. No one never seen him without it, 'cept me and that ranger. Half the folks here abouts came into the world with Doc catching them, and half went out holding Doc's hand."

"Me, boy? Not hardly! Never did become no doc."

"The scarf? Sure I got it. Over at my place. Keep it next to my handiron. Right next to Doc's big book on the mantle."

Chapter Five

THE WEARY OLD MAN FINISHED his story as he blinked into the bottom of his glass. With the timelessness of mind peculiar to the old, he drifted across the years as if reading from the inside of his wrinkled eyelids. His eyes had been closed through most of the story.

The youth off the trail waited for his companion's mind to meander back to their dirty table in the poor-man's saloon. All around was the salty smell of wild men, tobacco smoke, and sawdust.

"That be the whole of it, boy," the old man mumbled, returning slowly to the present and his empty glass. "Say you knew old Doc, did you?"

"No," Frank repeated. "My pa knew Doc. Way back when. Why do they call you Doc if you ain't never been schooled?"

"It's just them young ones funning me. They don't mean no harm, though. To the old folks 'round here, I'm still called Doc 'cause of all I learnt from the real Doc what I told you about. I have sewed up my share of bodies, I can tell you that, for sure. But I ain't no doctor." The old man sighed deeply and his shoulders slouched. "Sure don't mind being called Doc." Tears twinkled in the fine old eyes slightly bloodshot from warm beer. He sniffed, laid his empty glass down hard on the table, and looked across at his youthful company.

"One more, barkeep," Frank shouted.

"Thanks, boy," the old man smiled as another glass was laid upon the gritty table. "Say you be headed south?"

"South. Yes. Got my stores being packed at the mercantile. Animal's at the livery. I guess I should be on my way."

The old man laid his empty glass down. He looked hard at his wrinkled hands on the tabletop and he licked his lips. Frank waited patiently for the old man to collect his next thought.

"Maybe, boy, you have use for someone who can bleed a vein and stitch a wound? I know horses, too." When the old man looked squarely into the youth's clean face, Frank was stunned by the sudden clarity in the pale eyes.

"Don't know . . . Doc. We're five already."

"Be less than that after Cedar City, I'd say. Besides, I still carry my own weight. Got my handiron, too. It'll take a cap and ball right now. I keep it well cleaned and oiled."

The youth thought of the month of hard trail still ahead and of its perils. It was all that the young man could handle. And the old man looked used up. But he also thought about growing old alone, in a cheap saloon at an unkind table in the corner.

"You got a mount?"

"The best, boy! Like me: old and hard."

"Then fetch your iron, Doc."

"Done."

"I'll meet you at the livery. I'll stop at the mercantile on the way."

"Say, what will your friends say when you ride in with me?"

"I'll tell 'em we need a doc."

Frank stood and pushed his chair aside which made little tracks in the sawdust. When the old man rose, he was not slouching. The old man was taller than Frank, although thick in the middle. On his way out, Doc laid his dirty glass on the bar. "Keep it," he smiled. "Going south."

In the general store, Frank found his trail stores tightly bound to fit over a saddle back. After paying the merchant, the horseman slung the sack of necessaries over his shoulder for the trek to the livery.

Doc was already at the livery, waiting and mounted. His saddle was surprisingly well oiled and hand-rubbed until it glowed with the patina of fine leather. His horse was a mousy brown, but well muscled, broad of chest and girth, with sturdy short cannon bones. The old man wore a light duster that reached down to his tattered boots and spurs. The long duster was pulled aside to reveal an old handiron, also well oiled. In the sunshine, rising heat from the dirt street thinned the dry air which muffled the din of people and wagons.

The youth nodded his approval up to the smiling gray eyes under a broad-brimmed hat. Doc returned the nod toward the young man's fine new hat with its four creases and hard point.

Over his shoulder aching from the feed sack, Frank saw the smithy lead his horse from the stifling barn. The big horse flared his nostrils to the fresh, calm air. One night of clean straw bedding, fresh water, and quality oats had worked the trail soreness from the mount's shining flanks and high withers. The animal pressed his fuzzy nose into Frank's neck with familial greeting.

"Morning, old salt," the youth smiled, rubbing the animal's whiskered muzzle. The horse blinked an equine greeting with his large black eyes.

"Old Doc riding with you, boy?" the liveryman called, holding a hand up against the fierce sun. The boy detected something of a laugh in the sweating blacksmith's voice.

"Reckon so," Doc answered for Frank. The rider's face was hard.

The smithy only grunted his opinion of the youth's judgment. Doc gently squeezed his animal's sides and the restless mount moved impatiently into his bit and pawed the dusty earth.

"Thanks," Frank said as he flipped a coin into the smithy's huge hand. The liveryman spat a ribbon of black chew toward the fetlocks of the boy's animal. Without another word, the dirty man disappeared into his humid world of red hot iron and air heavy with ammonia vapors simmering up from pools of horse urine.

When the youngest of the Hart Brothers reined his mount onto the dusty street, Doc matched his easy pace. The two riders laden with supplies rode slowly westward down the main street of Fort Smith.

Over their right shoulders to the north, the green mountains reached for the clear purple sky. With their animals equal in height at the shoulder, Doc rode ramrod straight with a deep cavalry seat and long stirrup leathers. His shoulders were braced well back with his hips rocking in perfect tempo with the slow pace of the animals' walk. From the corner of his eye, the youth watched Doc ride with his eyes cast deliberately ahead. Doc avoided the many eyes that stopped to study the two departing riders: the youthful stranger come and gone in a day, and the old man come and gone in sixty odd years. Doc rode with his right hand resting lightly on the iron bulge at his hip.

In the fierce daylight, Doc savored every second of his leaving the squalid outpost retreating in the dust rising from eight hooves. His squinting eyes did not linger on the rotted skeleton of the ancient livery where he had first set eyes on a frontier physician half a century earlier. Nothing stood on the baked mud where once a dress shop had stairs leading up to a long-gone surgeon's office. He rode slowly past the poor-man's saloon where everyone inside knew which table was "Doc's." That table waited empty. When at last the street with its wagon ruts and clapboard buildings entered the haze of dust behind the two riders, the old man smiled with deep lines breaking his leather face.

At Doc's side, the youth sighed with relief that his brief passage into town had ended without incident and without challenges from the street. Open country relieved the riders' fear of dark alleys and the sheriff's narrow eyes.

All afternoon they rode. Green mountains rose around them as they aimed toward the camp of Frank's kin and the brittle company of the blackclad Deacon. When the white sun burned through evening haze along far western peaks, the trail thickened with brambles, aged firs, and craggy streams of white water.

"There," Frank pointed. "By them stumps."

Doc rode easily toward a dense thicket. Thinly pointed treetops obscured the darkening sky. Along a narrow trail only one horse wide, the pair rode single

file into the dusky vines. Where a shallow stream cut
through the trail, Frank left the dirt road for the trees.
His animal lowered his face to watch the dangerous
ground along a narrow switchback.

The riders carefully eased their horses down a hill-
side. The animals slid down with their hind hocks
touching the slick grassy incline. At bottom, the two
horses broke into a short trot.

Among thin pines, the two tired riders found four
horses secured to a crosstie: three well-worn mounts
and the towering gray of the Deacon. The two riders
dismounted stiffly. Among the trees, eight eyeballs
squinted over four raised revolvers with the hammers
eared back.

Chapter Six

"NICE HAT, LITTLE BROTHER," A deep voice called from the cover of trees.

"Thanks," laughed the youngest brother who spoke into the air as he dismounted and walked toward a hitching rope where he secured his horse. At his side, Doc did the same.

From the trees, the oldest brother emerged, followed by the two middle brothers and the Deacon. The four men returned their handirons to leather as they closely studied the dishevelled old man standing close to the brother with the new Montana peak hat.

"This here is Doc," Frank smiled. His voice was heavy with exhaustion. Trail dust outlined dark rivulets of sweat on his smooth face. "Doc will be riding south with us if there be no objection."

Doc shifted his weight on legs trembling from fatigue. The company of strangers made him uncomfortable.

"Coffee is still hot," was the greeting from the oldest brother who nodded toward Doc. Since the little band only built fires in daylight, the tin coffee pot sat cooling on the warm stones of the extinguished firepit. Men of the wild waste few words and Doc smiled silently. He and Frank unsaddled their horses.

45

Doc swayed on weary old legs that carried him toward a fallen timber beside the warm firepit. The other men joined him in the gathering darkness.

The six salty men took their places sitting on logs and stumps. They slouched around the warm hole in the green sod where the coffee pot filled the night air with warm smells of home. The Deacon kept his distance from the four brothers and Doc. Behind them, six animals munched the sparse grass of the ravine.

"How was town, little brother?" red-bearded Luke asked.

"A real hoot," Frank smiled from behind his tin cup of warm coffee. "I did behave myself."

"Bet you did," Jason said. His salt and pepper beard concealed a grin.

Doc and the youngest shootist washed the trail dust down with warm coffee. Around them, the night chill brought up a fine fog from the damp earth covered with pine needles. Behind them, a creek gurgled peacefully.

By the time the coffee was gone, the gorge was black. Overhead, a thousand stars twinkled brightly in the thin mountain air. One by one, each man glanced upward and silently took the measure of the wide, cold sky. Squinting eyes distinguished red stars from blue. To men of the wild, night is as familiar as the well-worn creases of their bedrolls.

"Reckon the horses are rested enough," the Deacon sighed after an hour of sitting on hard timbers. The Deacon's tall gray horse heard his master's voice. The animal pawed the earth as if the hard steed were ready to feel the trail underfoot.

The six men rose to saddle up. Frank and Doc walked the slowest. Their legs still ached from the trail behind them. Each had to rub his thighs to muster the energy to move. Jason watched his little brother hobble toward his mount. The bare back of the tired horse showed the outline of the youth's saddle etched in dusty, horse sweat. Frank dragged his battered saddle.

"We have to travel at night so close to town," Jason said softly. He felt the pain of their youngest.

"Seems so," Frank muttered.

After cinching their saddles tight, six mounted riders slowly climbed the steep trail. Frank and Doc took the lead to prevent their tired horses from straggling too far behind in the darkness. Frank squinted to see pine branches before he ate them. Doc followed with his chin resting on his chest. At least the chilly air soothed their wind-burned faces.

Through the damp darkness, they rode close to the white water of the narrow Bear River.

BY THE TIME the eastern sky became pink, the horses walked heavily and their hooves barely left the ground. Their ironshod feet dragged through the dust and left little skid marks of fatigue. Only the Deacon's proud animal carried his head high with the haughty grandeur of an Arabian stallion.

In the gray dawn, the distant rumble of horses on the trail alerted the company riding single file beneath the pines. The riders stiffened their backs and tightened their weak legs on their animals' flanks. They reined their mounts into the dense stand of trees close to the trail.

They stopped within the cover of the trees far from the trail. They could not see the road when they dismounted beside a small creek. The six lathered horses nudged toward the clear water. The placid stream looked gray under gray sky. Five animals dropped their sweating faces to drink. The Deacon's horse stood quietly aside waiting his turn to drink alone like his master.

The riders sat quietly on stumps and cocked their ears toward the trail on the far side of the trees. Several mounted men pounded down the trail. A wagon followed and then more riders.

The traffic nearby made the hidden band uneasy so close to another tiny town.

"Big doings in town today," Frank mumbled as he wiped his face. Exhaustion weakened his voice to a dry rasp.

"Too bad we don't have an invite," the Deacon said coldly.

As the white sun rose in a purple sky, the six men camped beside the river surrounded by lush firs. By daylight, they grained their animals from the stores fetched by the youth. They took care to find the driest kindling for their fire to avoid making smoke under the coffee pot.

The unsaddled animals sucked up the fresh oats like candy before lowering their heads to the poor grass. While the sky blued and the earth warmed, each man tended quietly to his solitary business. The Deacon's black form lingered close to his horse. Frank flecked specs of dust from his new hat. At his side, Doc sat shining his Mexican spurs in his gnarled hands.

The day passed slowly and easily although the company tensed with each new wagon creaking down the winding road leading into town three miles away.

By the time another evening's ground fog simmered up from the soft floor of the forest, the sun was low in the west. As the fog thickened, the sounds from the trail and the nearby town hung longer on the misty air.

With the coming of evening twilight, the wet air carried a strange sound of iron beating dry wood. In town, there was serious building in progress. The unseen travelers on the dirt road galloped toward the clamor, which captivated the six listeners within the forest beside the dark water.

With all the traffic so close to their hiding place and with all of the noise coming from town, the six exhausted riders resolved to spend the cool night under cover rather than taking to the trail.

Chapter Seven

MUMFORD HENDERSON HATED HIS NAME. So he called himself Saguaro. "Saguaro, like the cactus: prickly and not to be trifled with," Mumford Henderson would say when asked about his wherefores.

"Grub's here, boy," the thick marshal mumbled around the butt of his black stogie. A trickle of black ooze leaked from the corner of his stubbled mouth toward his sweat-soaked collar.

"Obliged," sniffed the tall man who reached through the black iron bars for the tin plate and a steaming cup of coffee.

The marshal's hard hands passed the hot food through the bars. The keeper and the kept squinted at each other through a cloud of putrid breath hanging between them in the stale air of the humid cell.

"T'ain't much of a last meal, Marshal," grinned the caged man who hated his name.

"Guess not," the officer said as his dark tongue licked his upper lip in the sweltering heat.

The tiny town was a blemish on the rocky countryside. Rows of rundown buildings held the fine white dust of Main Street like a layer of light snow. Leaking from the barred window and from the wooden ceiling, a rain of dust covered the tattered shirt and patched trousers of Saguaro who paid no mind to the filth. Saguaro sat cross-legged on his dusty bunk. His dirty face was close to the plate of beans and mule meat.

"Eat up, boy," the marshal ordered softly.

"Mite gritty," Saguaro smiled into his tin plate of greasy stew.

"Fit for the likes of you, I'd say," the marshal grumbled.

The sticky night was filled with the justice of the West's hard places: heavy hammers driven by the clammy hands of the law. They beat hand-forged nails into a high wooden stage through which the man who hated his name would drop with dawn's humid light. Beneath Saguaro's boots, the pounding could be felt through the hard ground. Along with the noise from the new scaffold, smaller hammers rang dully where shopkeepers boarded their windows against the throng that at first light, would assemble to do God's work after singing His praises. From the mountainous countryside, hungry men brought their hungry women and children down the steep trails to enjoy the morning carnival and its hawkers of snake oil medicinals.

"Noisy, ain't it, Marshal?" slurped the condemned man behind his bars.

"Not for long," the lawman stammered. "Be real quiet for you soon enough, boy."

"Seems so," Saguaro grinned. Ten days earlier that same tight smile had been the last sight seen by two nameless drifters. Then, at the feet of the thin man who now ate his last meal, they had eaten the dusty street that soaked up their dark blood.

The marshal stuffed his body into a chair behind a small table near the prisoner's cage. The marshal's boots touched the top of the table and nudged a lantern that sent oily smoke toward the ceiling. The hammering outside stopped. The marshal's belly jerked when the sudden silence was broken by the crashing of the stagedoor outside. A heavy sandbag dangled at the end of a twisting rope. In the darkness, men clapped loudly at the hanging of a fifty-pound sack of sand, which turned silently beside the swaying trapdoor. Hammering resumed and the marshal toyed with his heavy Peacemaker handiron. He laid the black revolver on top of the table where his legs rested.

"Thanks," smiled Saguaro who slid his dry plate under the bars and across the floor as far as he could reach. The marshal's chair tipped backward until the front legs lifted from the dusty floor.

Before the marshal could respond, the heavy sandbag again crashed through the trapdoor and stopped in midair. The sagging lawman closed his eyes and the yellow lantern light glistened on his eyelids.

"Been marshaling long?" Saguaro asked from his mattress.

"Forever, seems like," the marshal answered thickly as if from sleep. With his eyes closed, the thick man's voice lost its coldness. "Since can't remember when. All my life."

"How long's that, Marshal?"

"Wadya say, boy?"

"Said, 'How long's that,' what you been a lawman?"

The marshal stirred and his chair creaked with its front legs still airborne.

"Going on forty years. Since I deputied with the marshal before me. I was fifteen years old then. That marshal has been in the ground thirty years." The marshal's many chins rested on his soiled collar.

"Long time."

"Guess so, boy," the lawman mumbled. His eyes were still closed. "How long you been thieving?"

"I ain't never took what weren't mine! That's a fact." The sweating man in the cage straightened his back against the wall.

"Don't matter, boy. They ain't hanging you for stealing come daybreak."

"Them what I plugged laid hands on me, Marshal. It weren't no cold-blooded killing at all. You was there! You saw it! I just filled my hand the faster. That was all." Saguaro spoke hoarsely through clenched teeth. "And they're gonna hang me for that!"

When Saguaro finished, his words trailed off. His passion drained what energy he had in the stifling heat.

"Well, boy, if the judge didn't know why you should swing, reckon that you do."

Saguaro said nothing. He knew well enough after a short but hard life.

"Must be law, boy. Law and order. When this territory is emptied of the likes of you, the Union Pacific railroad will come in and make this place a state."

The crash of the hanging sandbag filled the stuffy backroom of the jail. The dozing marshal said nothing but Saguaro squirmed and his legs dropped to the dusty floor. When his heels did not reach the rough-hewn flooring, he eased forward until his feet touched the ground. The prisoner moved his feet on the solid floor while outside the sandbag only touched the hot air.

Both men looked to the low doorway that opened into the gloom of the jail's outer office. A short, thin woman entered and her youthful firmness brought color to the dismal cellblock.

"Marybeth!" the marshal snapped. His chair rocked forward and his boots hit the floor. "This ain't no place for you, child."

The young woman stood before the marshal's sooty lantern. Saguaro gripped the iron bars framing his gaunt face. His knuckles were white and wet.

Marybeth glowed with rosy youth. Her long, light hair lay close to her clean face. Marybeth's clear blue eyes were the color of the sea after the rain.

"I want to see Saguaro. . . . You can't stop me, Marshal." The young woman spoke through perfect teeth.

"Reckon not, child."

"In private, Marshal."

Saguaro stood silently. His fingers were still white around the bars as the marshal gathered his thoughts.

"Alright, child. . . . Behave as if your daddy were here."

Marybeth always did. Saguaro had wished it were not so.

The cellblock door to the front office creaked closed as the marshal left the teenage woman and the prisoner. The heavy lawman carried the keys. His hand rested on the Peacemaker returned to his hip.

"You shouldn't have come here," Saguaro whispered with pain in his voice.

The haggard prisoner in his early twenties hated both his name and what had become of it. He shuffled from the bars toward the rear of his cage. He gulped the humid air and his words stuck to the brick wall before his thin face.

"Please, Marybeth. Go home. I don't want you to see what they do to me. I can die well if I'm alone." He turned his face to the woman whose eyes glowed close to the bars. "If you are nearby, I cannot die well. Please!"

"I want you to be free," the young woman said through her tears.

"What am I to do, Marybeth? There is so little time now."

He looked into her pale eyes full of anguish.

"Saguaro, I am with you now and always."

The woman reached under her skirt which dragged on the filthy floor. She pulled out a tiny Colt, Third Model .41 pistol small enough to fit in her palm.

"Be free," she whispered handing the small weapon to the wide-eyed prisoner. As Saguaro closed his fist around the iron, he flinched as another sandbag was lynched in the night.

"The marshal?" Saguaro breathed.

"The marshal has lived his life," she pleaded. "We have not."

"Marybeth, I never killed no man in cold blood. Never." Saguaro paced his narrow cell.

"You have to, Saguaro! I want us to be together. We have no other chance!"

The clean woman wept quietly with her forehead resting upon Saguaro's hand gripping the bars.

"Come to me, Saguaro. Please."

The woman kissed his dirty fingers. She turned quickly. Her skirt swept the floor as she pushed the door open and left the cellblock.

Saguaro waited a long time before the marshal returned to the backroom. The condemned man studied the thick lawman's face. The man who hated his own name buried the weapon inside his shirt that stuck to his sweating body.

"Be light soon, boy. Not much time."

Saguaro was taken by the calm in the big man's voice. His words carried a strange quietude.

"No. Not much time," the marshal repeated as he squinted outside toward the carpenters. "There ain't no need to keep that up all damn night!" The lawman shouted through the barred window.

The marshal turned toward his prisoner.

"Reckon anyone who's cared for by that child ain't all bad."

"Guess not, Marshal." Saguaro was comforted by the thought.

The officer returned to his chair at the cluttered desk. Beside the oil lamp, he laid the heavy Peacemaker. Its battered walnut grip lay near the big man's hand. The weary marshal rested his double chin on his dirty shirt.

"You'll be my last dispatching, boy," the marshal said softly. His eyes remained closed and he spoke to the humid air. "Think I'll hang up my irons come winter. Enough fighting and killing for one lifetime. Yessir. Hang 'em up for good."

Saguaro listened to the lawman's strange monologue. The prisoner felt the little derringer warm inside his shirt.

"Marshal?"

"Boy?"

"Not like me, you know, to go out without a fight."

"I wouldn't either, Saguaro," the drooping man whispered.

Saguaro could not recall the marshal using his name before.

"Reckon not, Marshal," sighed the thin man behind the bars.

For a silent hour, the lamp flickered and the marshal dozed in his chair. Like the cheeks of the anguished girl standing away from the growing crowd in the dark street, the eastern sky was barely pink behind the black frocked men standing atop the spindly wooden tower on the town square.

"Best make your peace, boy," the marshal said, turning a gold pocket watch over in his hard hand. Saguaro stirred anxiously when the lawman pushed back from his desk and stood. When the marshal blew out the little lantern, he shoved his Peacemaker into his hip holster.

Saguaro was stunned to see the squalid room faintly lighted from the barred window. He suddenly felt his bowels turn to water.

"Be outside a minute, boy," the marshal said softly. "Make your peace, son."

Standing outside on the wooden stoop of his office, the lawman squinted into the dawn toward the scaffold. On the high platform above the thirteenth step, two large deputies stood close to a parson in white collar. The parson's face looked as if all of the blood had been drained out. In his ashen hands, he fumbled with a small book.

Across the square filled with gawking citizens, the blue-eyed girl frowned when her eyes met the blank stare of the marshal. The lawman turned from the tear-stained face and entered his jailhouse.

The milling crowd in the dirt street murmured. They advanced like a red-eyed animal toward the steps of the jail. The pitch of their clamor increased as the clear sky brightened.

Like a thunderbolt, the crack of a tiny handiron rolled through the open bars toward the crowd. The mass stopped in its tracks. The men atop the death tower turned toward the jail. Across the street, a young woman with eyes running like water clutched her hands to her heart. She did not breathe when the hushed mob reached the jail door.

There was no sound in the square. A hawk circled the crowd before climbing into the purple morning sky.

When the marshal squeezed his thick body through the doorway, the throng divided silently to let him pass. The tall man walked slowly across the square. He did not pause when he passed the breathless woman whose face was streaked with a child's hot tears.

Only the grieving woman with shining eyes noted that the marshal did not carry the terrible weight of an iron star on his wet shirt. He had proudly worn the badge for all of his adult life.

Chapter Eight

A MAN DOES A CERTAIN dance when his bare foot finds a scorpion inside his boot. He is not apt to forget it. Luke pounded his overturned boot before putting his foot inside. His brothers laughed at their mutual memory of another camp on the high plains.

While the four brothers chuckled quietly, Doc shuffled slowly toward his horse secured to the rope crosstie between two trees. The animal scratched his rump against a fat pine tree.

The western sky was red with sunset following the company's day-long rest.

The solitary Deacon marched through fog rising from the cooling earth between the tall trees. He carried his mount's bridle leathers. The Deacon's fine saddle was already cinched to his animal. The tall horse obediently lowered his royal face to take the bit which the Deacon first warmed between his hands. Close by, the four brothers and Doc tacked their mounts for the nighttime ride. On the far side of their tree-lined camp, the day's steady traffic of wagons along the road had ebbed to an occasional buggy or rider.

In the gathering darkness, Luke, Frank, Samuel and Doc were busy cinching their saddles tight. Jason and the Deacon stood nervously beside their horses. The Deacon rested his right hand on the revolver at his hip and his narrow eyes scanned the trees bordering their clearing. Jason squinted warily into the darkening stand of trees and he felt the familiar itch at the back of his neck. His shooting hand dropped silently to his hip iron.

"Evening, boys." A deep and calm voice came from the black trees.

The shock of the greeting from the darkness struck the camp like ball lightning which can knock a man stone dead and smoking from the saddle.

Only the eye of a treebound hawk was quick enough to follow the speed of the oldest brother and the Deacon clearing leather together. Each shootist squinted over his raised handiron toward the trees. The peculiar tranquility of the stranger's voice froze the two trigger-fingers poised to blow down the saplings with hot lead.

"Easy, boys," soothed the voice from the trees. "Easy now."

The brothers, Doc, and the Deacon faced the trees.

"Come on in with your hands on your head," the Deacon called coldly.

From the trees, the wide frame of the marshal walked slowly into the camp illuminated by the last of daylight which pierced the forest. The stranger led his animal by its loose reins.

"No need for them irons," the round and sweating face smiled uneasily. The man and his horse stopped beside the cold firepit.

The big man's bone-weary face inspired Jason to ear down the hammer of his revolver. He pushed the Remington into his holster. The Deacon lowered his weapon, but he held it with the hammer cocked beside his hip.

"Just coming in for that there spring water. Me and the horse is dry." The man moved toward the water where the animal lowered his dusty face. All eyes settled on the only clean spot on the tall stranger's tattered blouse: a star shaped, bright spot where the linen was not faded. The Deacon's eyes could make out two tiny holes on the figure where the badge's pin had held the star in place. The residue of the star held the Deacon's attention.

"Evening, Sheriff," said the Deacon with hard words.

"Marshal, actually. Recently retired," the new man sighed.

The marshal led his mount from the creek.

"Where you boys headed?"

"South," Jason and the Deacon replied together. The Deacon repeated "South" alone, to assert his leadership.

"Cedar City," the marshal said as if stating a fact.

"The rendezvous," Frank said cheerfully.

The marshal nodded and lowered his head. He knew the likes of those headed for the rendezvous. He had thrown many of them out of his little town half a day's ride away.

Without a word, the Deacon slid his piece into the holster under his waistcoat.

"Can you boys use another iron between here and Cedar City?" The marshal looked squarely into the Deacon's face. He already knew who led the company of gunmen.

"The last swallow of coffee is hot," the youngest brother offered the stranger.

"Thanks. I'm really dry." The marshal handed the reins of his mount to Frank before making his way in the dark to the cooling firepit where the tin pot sat.

"And then we move," the Deacon ordered forcefully. He stroked the firm neck of his horse which pawed the ground.

While the marshal drank the last of the gritty coffee, the brothers gathered their stores and horse tack. The lawman's horse sighed deeply when his rider mounted his weary back.

DOWN THE SALT Lake Cutoff, the riders made their slow way through Mormon country of the Utah territory.

Dry-camping by day and moving southward by night, the dusty troop of seven riders skirted the isolated outposts of white men along the Overland Trail. The trail of wagon wheel ruts stretched toward Ogden and Provo beside the brackish estuaries of the Great Salt Lake.

The days of concealed campsites and cold nights in the saddle became weeks of eating trail dust. The four brothers kept to their own company with Doc riding at Frank's elbow. The Deacon and the marshal each kept to himself. Although each rider's knees were blue and raw inside their nighttime woollies, only Doc prospered from the grueling monotony.

Doc seemed to grow stronger as the searing heat of the day and the black chill of the night trail invigorated his old bones. The trail washed away from Doc the flaccidness of his lifelong captivity in the stuffy town. His back became straight and his old hands moved calmly with the rocking gait of his hard mount. By day, Frank kept close to Doc.

When the four brothers spoke quietly among themselves, they spoke of home and of better times. The Deacon spoke only to his arrogant mount. Doc and the shabby marshal spoke easily of their pasts where pipe dreams and barren reality melded into one in the memories of old men.

The marshal rode at the rear of the company. He kept to his own memories of the hanging tree where he spent his life in the Law doing the work of little men too callow to soil their own pale hands. The rumpled lawman slept fitfully, if he slept at all.

Camping by day near Provo, the riders dispatched the Deacon into town to gather supplies. They knew that the Deacon would not tarry and that he would ride back alone.

SOUTH OF SPANISH Fork, the green to the west became brown. By tiny Yuba Lake, they camped three days to rest the animals and their own legs sore and raw. On the fourth night in camp, the company tacked their horses freshly rested.

In the darkening twilight, the first bullet lifted the Deacon's fine hat from his head a heartbeat before the roar of a rifle exploded.

The shaken Deacon dove for the ground. Snaking his hands to his hips and his twin irons, he looked upward to the dense trees. Another burst of red embers followed a rifle ball from the trees. The Deacon's flashing revolvers made a rain of pine needles.

Beside the Deacon, the four brothers hugged the earth. Behind them, Doc stood behind his trembling horse and fired his handiron into the patch of trees drawing the Deacon's fire.

For a full minute, hot weapons fired into the clearing of the campsite. The seven horsemen laid back the saplings with their return fire. Splinters of pine whistled through the smoky air.

From the swirling smoke of the trees, first one cry of pain then another joined the volley of gunfire.

With the suddenness of its opening fury, the musketry from the trees stopped. With a final report from the Deacon's revolver, the fusillade ended. Only moaning from the nearby trees broke the silence. Terrified horses pulled frantically at their restraining leathers secured to a crosstie.

A twig snapped and a shadow stumbled from the trees into the dark campsite. The gray outline of a man clutched wildly at his chest where a watery gurgle of bloody air bubbled through red fingers. The ripped lungs dripped frothy blood as the Deacon's white knuckles raised his cocked handiron.

Before the Deacon could finish the lungshot intruder, the darkness glowed again. A rifle sent a ball into the forehead of the frantic shadow. The skull at the hairline exploded with a splash of gray meat and yellow bone. The stranger collapsed heavily into a heap across the cold firepit.

Behind the prone riders, the figure with the smoking rifle stood with his legs wide apart. All eyes squinted at the stranger who rested his buffalo rifle atop his boot. He stood calmly.

The stranger looked into seven weapons pointed at

his chest and face.

"Lay it down easy," the Deacon ordered as he rose from the soft floor of the forest camp. "Light the fire, boy," the Deacon hissed at the youngest brother.

The nervous men climbed to their feet and closed in slowly around the stranger. Frank knelt at the cold firepit bathed in black blood draining from the head of the dead highwayman. The brother lit dry twigs and a small flame rolled along the kindling.

Firelight pushed back the darkness until the seven travelers could see the man standing next to his rifle which lay in the damp grass. The light opened the little clearing. Just at the edge, two figures lay face down.

Seven pairs of narrow eyes studied the stranger who straddled his rifle. The man looked calmly about the camp and at the men breathing hard into his face. The intruder who had appeared in time to destroy the last attacker wore the regalia of the mountain men: soft leather leggings and long trail duster, fur hat, and a long greasy beard. The Deacon studied the stranger's rifle on the ground: an aged, browned Hawken rifle, stoked with black powder and patched, roundball. At the stranger's side dangled his "possibles" pouch stuffed with caps and hand-cast lead balls. A brass powder flask hung from his other shoulder.

"What's your name," the Deacon ordered over his raised revolver.

The stranger blinked back at the Deacon with one eye. His left eye was hidden behind a buckskin patch. A single pink scar ran down his dirty forehead, behind the brown patch, and stopped at the line of his coarse beard. The one useful eye was dark and squinting. The expression on the half-blind and gritty face suggested that there was not much behind it.

"Your name?" The Deacon had to switch his heavy weapon to his left hand.

"No Account, now. Don't remember my city name no more."

Chapter Nine

WITH THE STRANGER STANDING IN the center of the clearing, the company moved restlessly in and out of the firelight to prepare for the night ride. No one left the fireside until he had first reloaded his handiron and had twirled the primed cylinder at eye level.

"Oh, God!" came a dreadful wail from the darkness.

The voice of anguish was Luke's. The company spun with irons drawn to face the darkness where the voice called "Oh, no!"

The fire illuminated the contorted face of the big man advancing from the crosstie where the animals were secured. The deep lines in his face glistened with tears. No Account turned his back to the fire and the youngest brother let out a little yelp when his boot landed on the dead hand of the man whose brains sizzled at the base of the fire.

Jason laid his hand lightly on his grieving brother. He studied Luke for sign of a wound. No one spoke in the calm night air filled only with the fire's crackling and the bubbling of the broiling face beside the fire.

"Old hoss is plugged, Brother," the big man sobbed. "Hit clean through the brisket. Old boy be down by them trees." He pointed toward the edge of the darkness from which the snorting of the Deacon's gray could be heard. Close to the gray stallion lay a dead horse still tied.

Luke sat on a stump near the little fire. He hunched over with his elbows resting on his knees. His chin touched his chest.

The other men stood aside. Doc who knew death well enough, the marshal, No Account, three Hart Brothers, and even the stone face of the Deacon grieved silently. The firelight glistened at the corners of the Deacon's hard eyes.

They grieved for one of their own. In the wild, a man's horse is his companion, his trusted friend, his patient and sad-eyed listener to stories of home and kin which grow warmer with each retelling. And a man's mount is his last meal this side of Forever.

"What a good old salt," the big man said to the ground. "We burned a lot of daylight together, him and me. Carried me through more than one tight scrape. I could sleep in the saddle and he always knew the way, straight and true." Luke sighed deeply. He was finished mourning. There was work to do.

"Long walk south," Luke sniffed, wiping his face. He stood up and shook off his grief. But he felt no shame at his tears. A man is allowed tears for a good horse down. Within the grim fraternity of wild men bearing summer names and secret pasts, that much was certain.

Without a word, No Account walked into the darkness. He quickly returned to the fire and led a tall, chestnut horse saddled and bridled. The animal's last owner laid dead close to the fire.

"Sure ain't the same. But it beats walking," Luke smiled. "Thanks."

The big man stroked the animal's fine jaw and he laid his face against the white blaze on the mount's face. Large black eyes blinked warmly at the man. Luke sniffed the sweet musty smell of a clean horse and he rubbed the old boy's alert ears. The horse nuzzled the tall man's neck.

"Good fellow," the brother smiled, patting the red mane. "Easy now."

From the darkness, No Account walked his own mount, a mud-colored animal with dull eyes like his master.

"Let's ride," the Deacon ordered. He walked quickly toward his own horse and gently stroked the gray face.

No Account mounted his mangy horse. The heavy Hawken rifle lay across the saddle in No Account's lap.

Beside the fading fire, the dead intruder's blackened skull steamed at the ragged emptiness where the brain had been blown out.

"We're going South," growled the marshal atop his horse. He cast a white eye toward No Account.

"The rendezvous?" No Account mumbled.

"For sure," called the youngest brother mounting up.

"Me too," No Account grinned behind his wild and filthy beard. "My partner and me."

The riders each laid their right hands on their hand-irons when a thin man entered the clearing. He rode a horse which the others quickly pegged as an old plow horse: weak in the shoulders, strong in his hindquarters, and swaybacked in between. The animal tossed his head nervously, showing that he was barely broke for reining.

The dusty man looked freshly thrown, or worse. Both of his eyes were blackened. When he licked his upper lip, one front tooth was gone. In the darkness, his face appeared clean-shaven and either badly bruised or as sooty as No Account.

"He don't talk," No Account said softly as the rider inched closer to No Account's side.

THE BAND OF nighttime riders rode south along the rutted Overland Trail. The nine silent men and their tired mounts traveled single-file in the chill darkness. The troop kept No Account in the lead to keep his Hawken musket from their back sides. No Account's companion never said a word but kept so close to him that the Hawken poked his leg when their horses bumped.

When the trail approached Springville on the road to the Mormon Corridor toward the south, the riders left the trail and skirted the little town of "Saints" as the men of the trail called the Mormons. They passed Springville under cover of the darkness which protected them from their own kind.

FOR TWENTY DAYS they rested by day and rode by night. They had to make 250 miles. Progress was slow, steering their mounts over treacherous trail in darkness. In the night chill, the moon in clear skies illuminated them in eerie light and haunting shadows. A stumbling horse meant the trail was too rough to navigate by night so the horses were led by hand behind walking men. Each rider kept to his own thoughts and each sensed the squinting eyes of the man behind him.

Dry-camping in daylight was for soft chatter, hot coffee boiled over smokeless kindling, and sourdough biscuits. In such camps, men oiled their handirons while the marshal spat black tobacco which sizzled in the firepit.

In daylight, the marshal studied No Account's silent mate. He wore a floppy, wide-brimmed hat down low on his smooth face. The blackened eyes turned purple and then tan from the sun. His hair was too short to leak out of the hat which he wore awake and asleep. He was short and thin, looking weak in the company of the other hard men, even Doc. When the sun was just right, the eyes within the still swollen cheeks glinted a pale gray.

The marshal sensed in these hidden camps that the quiet stranger avoided the marshal's face. After a lifetime in the law, the retired officer did not bother to work his brain over the thousands of dirty faces that had looked out from cages at him or had tried to stare him down in the middle of streets with no names. If No Account's partner knew the marshal, the lawman no longer cared. The little man under the wide hat did not carry a weapon.

When talk warmed the day camps, words were of all-night women or yellow metal heavy in California streams. No Account said nothing and his partner said less. When the tobacco-spitting marshal broke his silence, he spoke of Cedar City and the invitation to all the West's shootists to come and be damned.

"MAYBE ANOTHER WEEK, at most," the marshal said between spits of black chew.

The troop day-camped beside a creek. They sat beside their animals, freshly watered after a night on the trail. The riders watered their mounts first, in case intruders required a hasty retreat deeper into the trees. From a tributary of the Sevier River where they rested, morning fog rose in the calm air. The riders sat wrapped in their blankets to keep out the dawn chill.

"Ten days," the Deacon responded without looking up from under his crisp, black hat. He sat on a stump where he spun the shining cylinder of his ivory-handled revolver.

"Wonder what we'll find at Cedar City?" Samuel asked. He spoke toward the earth where he rested.

"Probably a brass band," Frank laughed.

"And chorus girls lined up to shake our hands," Doc added with his eyes closed and with a smile on his stubbled face.

"Been a peck of years since I last seen the sheriff of Cedar City what put out the invite to every man-killer between Saint Joe and the sea." The former lawman shot a ribbon of black tobacco juice into the creek. Even in the morning chill, the marshal was sweating. "Good man, that one."

"Don't think the jailhouse in Cedar City will be big enough for everyone heading down there," Luke said. "Meanness on top of meanness."

"I don't imagine," the Deacon grinned, "they'll be too many left to lock up after the carnival starts."

They spent a peaceful day beside white water flowing over smooth rocks.

AFTER ANOTHER EIGHT days of nighttime travel, they camped in daylight beside Little Salt Lake. One day north of Cedar City, they rested close to the trail.

They watered the animals and filled the canteens

under a blistering sun. In the humid heat, No Account's stench was unbearable to all but No Account.

Camping close to the trail, every man kept his hand beside his handiron. No Account rested with his Hawken musket earred back to the half-cock.

They tensed when noon brought a wagon down the trail toward Cedar City. A black-frocked Mormon tipped his hat at the camping horsemen who nodded beside their mounts. The "saint" hurried his team past the campers.

"Making miles by day don't sit easy," the Deacon said to Jason. "Ain't safe."

The horses remained saddled for the stop beside the small lake. Another buckboard creaked down the trail.

"Might as well move on," the marshal spat.

Each man gave his shooting iron one final inspection before taking saddle.

For the first time in daylight, the nine horsemen rode down the Mormon Corridor which would widen into the main street of Cedar City, Utah Territory.

Wagons and mounted men passed them along the trail. The other traffic knew to make way for the nine dusty men. Overhead, the white sun burned the backs of their necks in the calm, hot air. Dust raised by their animals' feet was quickly sucked back to the parched earth.

Each man rode with his free hand resting on his hip iron as more passersby traveled the dirt road toward Cedar City. No Account's filthy hand rested on the hammer of the browned Hawken. The rifle's brass trigger-guard and brass patchbox on the stock were a flat black. Mountain men traditionally apply charcoal to the musket's shining brass to prevent the sun from glinting off the brass furniture which can give a man's hiding place away.

The blinding sun was shoulder high when Cedar City lay shimmering in the heat rising from the end of the month-long Overland Trail.

Where the road touched the edge of town, a battered and wind-burned livery stood at the edge of Main Street. Another rundown stable stood across the street. In the distance, citizens trailing little dust clouds shuffled in the street. Waves of heat rising from the dirt gave the pedestrians the illusion of wading through a watery dream.

In the lead, Jason and the Deacon stopped their mounts shoulder to shoulder. Only the town's dirty-faced children paid attention to the newest strangers coming down the Overland.

Pausing in the ferocious heat, the weary riders raised their faces to a great banner which hung motionless in the thin air above their heads. The wide cloth stretched limply across the road and was secured with ropes to each livery marking the end of the Overland Trail at Cedar City.

Black letters thick as a man's arm covered the banner with words reaching from one side of the street to the other:

"CEDAR CITY: WELCOME ASSASSINS AND ROAD SCUM"

The stony face of the black-vested Deacon cracked into a narrow smile.

"Seems we're expected."

Chapter Ten

THE DEACON'S ROOM IN THE Grand Hotel was stuffy from the heat. Like the Deacon, the room was orderly with not a nickknack out of its appointed place.

In the hours since arriving at Cedar City, the Deacon had taken a room on the third floor of the Grand which stood on Main Street. He was clean-shaven and wore a fresh shirt. His vest with its gold watch chain and his knee-length Prince Albert waistcoat were immaculate, like his face smelling of lilac water. No Account raised his dirty face to sniff the tall man's wake.

"You need a bath," the Deacon said toward the open window.

"Just got my room."

The Deacon sat down on the bed where his two revolvers, a short cleaning rod, and strips of patching cloth lay. After cleaning the weapons, each strip emerged from each barrel as clean as the Deacon's scrubbed hands.

"Anyone see you come in here?" the starched Deacon asked.

"No. Them others was at the bath house." No Account crossed his legs. He still wore his rancid buckskins.

"Wouldn't do you no harm," the Deacon nodded. The mountain man's leathers were rapidly overpowering the perfume on the tall shootist's tight face. "We couldn't talk on the trail. I didn't expect to see you until town here. Where'd you come from anyway?"

No Account closed his one good eye and seemed to be concentrating hard. When he opened his right eye, his sunburned forehead wrinkled. His words came slowly.

"Them bushwackers was after me. And the one I rode in with. They come on you first, is all."

"Why?" The Deacon turned from the window. He was suddenly angry. "You could have gotten all of us killed out there."

"I had something they wanted, I guess."

"What?"

"The one I rode with."

The Deacon was losing patience in the withering heat.

"I don't understand. Where is he, anyway?"

"Comfort Alley." No Account smiled.

"Couldn't he wait?"

"Ain't no 'he.' That's a woman."

"A woman?" The Deacon thought for a moment. "He—she—did seem to keep to herself."

"I found her. Them bushwackers had her. They done her. Four, maybe five they was."

"But why were they after you?"

"When I seen them doing her like that, I jumped them when they was done. Tied 'em up good. Then I gelded the one what broke her face. Ain't no reason to do her face like that." No Account's live eye creased and twinkled. "Guess they didn't take kindly to being gelded."

The Deacon looked hard at No Account.

"Did you have her, too?"

No Account squinted up at the tall man in black.

"Not when they're all broke up."

The Deacon nodded and his face softened. He reached into his vest and tossed a gold coin toward the mountain man.

"Well, you did right, I suppose. That's for Comfort Alley—when you smell better."

No Account picked up the coin and fumbled with the leather thong securing his possibles pouch of round-balls and percussion caps.

At the window, the tall man pushed a thin curtain aside to peer into the darkening street below.

"You can see it from here, opposite the courthouse," the Deacon said into the open window. "The Cattle-man's Bank and Trust. Got walls ten feet thick, they say. No one ever hit that damn place." The Deacon frowned into the humid twilight and pulled the curtain across the narrow window. He returned to the edge of the hard bed.

"What's your plan?" No Account leaned forward in his chair and glanced down at the Deacon's shining boots which had street and horse caked on the soles. The little man smiled at the touch of muck clinging to the dandy.

"I'll look the bank over first. Tomorrow, I'll deposit a bag at the Cattleman's. Take the lay of the land in there. I'll find its weak spots. If it has just one, we can take it." The Deacon did not smile.

"Tomorrow," No Account nodded. His beard opened around black teeth.

The Deacon moved to the room's second chair. When the man in black closed his eyes, No Account stood and walked to the door.

"Careful," the Deacon said softly without opening his eyes.

No Account said nothing. He eased the door open and poked his sweating neck into the hallway. Seeing no one, he slipped quietly into the hall after closing the door softly behind him.

In the hallway, No Account's moccasins made no sound. He paused outside a closed door and listened.

"A real bed. . . . A damned real bed." From the hallway, No Account recognized the voice of Frank, the youngest Hart fresh from his bath.

"Take your boots off the bed," Jason ordered. "Ma learned you better than that."

Frank slid his feet to the floor. He stood and peeled off his trail clothes until he stood in the nighttime uniform of men of the trail: long johns and a hat. Jason in his long drawers stood by the window.

The oldest brother paced the floor. The brother's beard was newly trimmed and his woollies were clean.

"Don't know what feels better, the real bed or the bath and shave," smiled the reclining youth.

"Guess we're both about ten pounds lighter with the trail washed off. Them tubs looked like we washed the horses in them. But your shave, little brother, was a waste of good money." The oldest brother chuckled.

The youngest smiled.

"Got to start sometime. Getting here with my hair at all entitles me to shave. Whether I need it or not." The youth looked up at the white-washed ceiling. He closed his eyes and enjoyed his fine quarters.

Jason stood at the window and looked down to the quiet, dark street. Pale light from a nearby saloon fell on a few horses dozing at the hitching post.

"Wish I didn't feel that we were walking into a bit of a tight here," the older brother said into the night.

"A tight?"

"Yeah. All them shootists riding in here. . . . A powerful lot of lead in this town just waiting to part other folks' hair." The bearded brother released the curtain which fell against the open window. He turned to Frank resting on the large bed. "Hope we're not out of our class. That's all."

"That's our business, Jason."

"I know. But if the sheriff here has really put up the gold he says is stashed in the Cattleman's, the riffraff blowing in off the Overland will have blood in their eyes." The older man sat down in the chair beside the window. "Too many man-killers for one hole-in-the-wall town." He rubbed his bare feet on the thick carpet. "Tell you one thing: This is my last shoot. No more after this one. Seen too much killing for one lifetime. Yessir, when this here shoot is over and done, all of us—God willing—can go home. Maybe we'll even have some of the gold what's to go to the last men standing after the shootout. We could buy that bottom land near Pa's and parcel it up amongst us fair and even. On 500 acres each, we could all do well. What you say, little brother?"

From the wide bed, only snoring rose from under the fine Montana peak hat.

In the gloomy hall illuminated by two lamps, No Account listened at the door of the two brothers who would share the soft bed. He waited for the answer to the oldest brother's question. Hearing nothing more, No Account moved quickly down the hall to the next room where Luke and Samuel bunked together. Only snoring rumbled from the closed door.

No Account stopped at the door where Doc bunked with the marshal. He listened for the familiar voices.

Instead of Doc's clear voice, he heard the voice of a woman and then the voice of the marshal.

"How you take it, mister?" the woman asked. Looking down at his feet, No Account saw no light leak from under the door.

"Without talk, thanks," the marshal said softly.

No Account rubbed his belly in the hallway when he heard the bed creak.

After a time, No Account heard the woman speak.

"What's the likes of you doing here anyway, Marshal, with all this other scum off the trail? Leastwise, you say you're a lawman."

No Account strained to hear the big man's answer.

"A man should die doing something honorable." The marshal spoke softly. No Account heard a chew wad plink into a spittoon.

"You call the rendezvous blood bath 'honorable'?"

"We'll have to wait and see."

"Have you any young ones, Marshal?"

There was quiet for a long time.

"A man should die well, as if he had children."

When the bed began creaking again, No Account stepped sideways and opened the door to his own room.

A single oil lamp atop a small nightstand illuminated the room with flickering, yellow shadows. No Account's shoulder-length hair and unkempt beard made a wolf-like ghost follow him across the walls.

Standing in front of a long mirror, he pulled his buckskin tunic over his head. The light reflected by the wavy mirror turned to pink where the scar crossing behind his eyepatch continued down from his neck, beside his breastbone, and down to his waist where it stopped. The ragged, healed wound looked like a seam which held in his heart and bowels.

No Account blinked his right eye at his own face in the mirror. He looked at the reflection's scar and his fingers slowly followed the injury toward his belly. His dirty fingers stopped beside the scar's end near his navel. He made little circles over a black tattoo carved deeply into his flesh. The image was a bear paw the size of his fist.

"I am bear," No Account mumbled softly. He smiled at the power of it.

Standing half-naked in front of the mirror in the yellow gloom and stifling heat, his body perspired. His one eye blinked at the image of a white man bound hand, foot, and throat to a Cheyenne stake. The Cheyenne Dog Soldiers had used a bear claw to split him open down to his liver. When he refused to die, the warriors knew that his guardian spirit must be the bear. To the Cheyenne, the bear is sacred. They know the bear to be an incarnation of their dead ancestors. They would starve before killing a bear for its meat. So they let their white prisoner go. His medicine was too strong.

"I am bear," No Account nodded with his fingers circling the bear paw whittled into his side out of respect. He tried to remember more about it. But that part of his mind had grown too hard.

When a knock on the door awakened him from his standing dream, No Account laid his leather shirt onto the bed before opening the door to the hallway.

He blinked down at a small woman with a hard face and eyes like the sky above the high plains. He took two steps backward and the woman entered his room and pulled the door closed behind her.

The good eye labored to focus in the dim light. When he turned around to reach for the lamp to raise the wick, the woman stopped him.

"No," she said. No Account turned quickly when he heard the voice. He knew it.

"What? You?" He had last seen her in men's clothing on the bitter trail.

In a long, faded dress, she looked like a woman, except for her pale hair cut close to her head. When last he had seen her, she had kept her wide-brimmed hat low over her eyes.

No Account remembered his bare chest. He reached for his soft blouse on the bed.

"You don't need that." She pushed his arm back toward the bed where he dropped the shirt. She looked down at his old wound and squinted. "Who cut you?"

"I am bear," No Account stammered. "What do you want with me?"

"You saved me from the animals who done me over. You can do me, if you want."

"I . . . I ain't got but one gold eagle."

"I don't want your money."

No Account blinked and his eyepatch twitched over the hole where his left eye had been cut by a bear claw and strong medicine.

"It ain't right." He studied her face closely. He could taste her warm breath, she stood so near. The man could feel his heart pounding in his sweating neck.

Her face was tanned from the trail. Fine lines creased at the corners of her eyes. Even close to the oil lamp, her eyes seemed dull as if all the youth had been pounded out of them by hairy fists beside a road which had no name.

"I ain't even heard your name."

"Marybeth." She blinked and looked away. "I was Marybeth Hutchinson."

"Oh. Where did you get a dress?"

"The hookers give it to me. Said I could stay down with them. In the alley where the whores live." She turned her hard face back to his. "It's my first real job." Her little smile was quick and cold.

No Account raised his hand to his forehead. His mind was befuddled by cheap whiskey and by a beating with coup sticks long ago.

"You ain't much more than a child. I ain't done no children." His liquor breath blew into her face in short, humid bursts.

"I'm grow'd."

Marybeth's small hands went to her throat where she began unbuttoning her collar. She continued slowly until her faded dress was open to the waist. With a shake of her shoulders, the dress fell around her into a pile at her shoes. No Account breathed hard. His right eye squinted at the white skin pushed out of the top of her tight bodice. Her underclothes were old and yellowed. The bare-chested mountain man turned his head toward the wall. But he faced the mirror filled with the woman in petticoats.

"Look at me," she said softly.

He wanted to look at the floor or at the closed door. But he had to look at the woman.

"I'm grow'd." She unbuttoned the bodice. No Account's remaining eye was wide when she put a hand under each of her naked breasts. The lamp light glistened on her skin.

The man's eyeball hurt as it dried from not blinking.

"You can have these. For free. I want to wash you first. Then you can do me." When she sighed, her eyes were suddenly shining. "All you have to do is promise me that you will shoot that marshal who rode in with us." She pulled down her petticoat layers and stepped out of the pile of old clothes. She wore nothing but her shoes. "That's all you have to do."

Chapter Eleven

THREE DAYS BEFORE THE CEDAR City rendezvous, Tuesday morning came hard with a fierce white sun in an empty sky.

The thin air rang with the music of heel chains jingling on silver spurs on the town's wooden sidewalks. Gaggles of children swarmed like sweating bees in the dusty streets. From a safe distance, packs of them followed at the spurred heels of the solitary strangers coming off the Overland by ones and twos. The mysterious shootists with heavy irons low on their hips were a holiday adventure.

"Like to examine the facilities first, if you please," said the Deacon immaculate in his knee-length waistcoat. The long black coat parted to treat the wide-eyed cashier to the crisp vest with its gold watch chain and two hand-irons with ivory grips.

"Certainly, sir," the lanky young man beamed from behind his caged, tellers' window.

"Obliged, son." The Deacon smiled with excessive courtesy.

"This way, sir." The youth pushed through the swinging half-doors separating his station from the main foyer of the Cattleman's Bank and Trust. The young man wore white sleeves held above his forearms with garters. He walked with the stooped back of one born to labor at white man's work far away from wind and sunshine.

"Thompson is my name, sir," the teller smiled over his shoulder as he led the Deacon toward the rear of the wide mezzanine. "Didn't catch your name, sir."

"I'll follow," the Deacon replied.

The pair walked behind the dozen young men stooped over their little cages where they sorted Federal notes and coin with the precision of riverboat gamblers. The Deacon felt their gaze upon his back as he walked with his hands laying upon the bulges inside his coat at each hip.

"It is a veritable fortress of stone and iron, I can assure you, sir," said the youth who led the Deacon to the rearmost corner of the airy bank. The Deacon glanced up toward the high ceiling ringed with great murals wall to wall. The colorful paintings depicted scenes of mighty railroads, great fields of grain, and bronzed men walking behind plows. The Deacon paused to look up.

"It's called 'Conquering the Great West,'" the youth said proudly. "Like I said: a fortress."

"Now that's a comfort," the Deacon nodded at the youth's shoulder.

"This way, sir."

They brushed past two hairy guards, each holding a rifle in his hands. A heavy Remington hung on each man's wide hip. They stood at either side of a massive wooden door with a steel lock mechanism. The guards with narrow eyes studied the Deacon. The teller pulled the brass latch and heaved open the door which creaked like a tomb. They entered another chamber. One wall contained an iron safe built into solid rock.

The Deacon blinked inside the stone vault. He inhaled the sweet vapors from two oil lamps which the youth kindled with a match.

"Stone walls five feet thick, sir. Even the floor and ceiling are stone blocks the size of buggies. An army could not break into here." The young teller's voice carried the thrill of a new father showing off his firstborn.

"It will hold my coin well enough," the Deacon nodded with a smile which unnerved the teller with its coldness.

"Then if you would follow me outside, sir." The banker gestured past the guards armed to their unsmiling teeth. He shoved the door closed and spun the round, iron handle on the door. Returning to the bank's business side, the Deacon squinted against the blinding daylight streaming in from the high glass windows with barred panes.

The youth returned to his cage behind the bars. The Deacon took his place on the far side.

"I'll just deposit this in your fine fortress for the moment, Mr. Thompson." The Deacon dug into his pocket and retrieved two bags of coin. The teller raised an eyebrow at the small sacks of gold.

"There's much more, Mr. Thompson. But I wanted to scout the place first. Had to make sure it was safe and secure."

"Very fine, sir. What name should I record for your vault box?"

"Just remember my face, Mr. Thompson. When I need to make a withdrawal, I'll ask for you."

The teller swallowed hard as he collected and tagged the big man's treasure. The Deacon touched the corner of his broad hat and turned slowly to leave.

Outside, the painfully bright sun pounded the Deacon's wrinkled neck as he marched briskly toward the livery. He walked head-down so his fine black hat could shield his pale eyes.

Looking at the dust rising from his spurred boots, the Deacon stopped short just a step from the sidewalk planks. A bullet of black ooze raised a tiny dust cloud at his feet. He held his boot slightly airborne above the tobacco spittle soaking into the dry ground. Without raising his face, the Deacon lowered his boot to the side of the little puddle of brown.

"Morning, Marshal," the Deacon said dryly without raising his face. "Up early, ain't you?"

"Early to rise," the marshal mumbled on the wooden walkway. The round man's clean shirt was already pockmarked with tobacco drool. He leaned on a whitewashed storefront in the shade of an over-hanging roof. The Deacon looked up at the marshal.

They looked into each other's eyes. The marshal's arms were crossed on his tobacco-stained shirt. His hands were well above his sidearm.

"Wanted to make a deposit and beat the crowd," the Deacon said softly. "No crime in that." He glanced up at the marshal's swollen cheek primed to fire again.

"No crime that I can see," smiled the man on the sidewalk. He unloaded another ribbon of chew far from the Deacon's feet. "Figure you only have another three days to complete your banking business."

Behind the Deacon, buckboards and men on horseback brought the sleepy town to life in the morning heat.

"Ain't really none of your business, is it?"

"Not yet, it ain't."

"Besides, Marshal," the Deacon choked on the last

word. "You don't wear the tin star no more."

"Not anymore," the marshal sighed. The big man's face locked for an instant on the Deacon's cold gray eyes.

When the Deacon turned abruptly to walk away, he heard a shot of chew thud into the street at his heels. He did not turn around when he heard the marshal's spurs jingling on the sidewalk.

The Deacon walked up the dirt street toward the stable. Passersby gave him a wide berth as they did for all of his kind.

Turning a corner, the Deacon heard the hard voices of hungry men and the strained laughter of women. Pausing in the sunshine at Comfort Alley, he looked down a dirt street filled with trail riffraff in tattered dusters and clusters of painted women in bright dresses. Their hems fluttered across piles of horse manure, loose and green from animals unaccustomed to their suddenly rich diet of decent grass and rolled oats.

One young woman with short blonde hair caught his narrow eyes. She seemed to stand out from the crowd of women talking business with the gunmen who were all strangers to the townfolk. The prositutes had answered the sheriff's call to the rendezvous, drawn by the pickings of Cedar City filled with shootists weighed down by heavy pockets and an urgent need for by-the-hour comfort.

The young woman squinted half a block toward the Deacon, blinked, and turned away. The tall man lowered his eyes and walked on. He imaged that he had seen those pale desperate eyes before. But his mind was too full of the Cattleman's Bank to think about her for long.

Reaching the livery from which hung the welcoming banner, he entered the cool gloom smelling strongly of horse urine and green manure.

All four brothers and Doc were already in the livery.

"Morning," the youngest brother smiled after a good night's sleep in a real bed.

The Deacon nodded curtly. He went directly to his animal which snorted a horse greeting to his master. The gray horse stuck his whiskered nose and fine jaw over the half-door to nuzzle the Deacon.

"Good old salt," the Deacon smiled with genuine kindness. The tall horse was the only living thing to whom the black-frocked shootist could turn his back with confidence.

"Seems everyone is up early today," Doc smiled uneasily. Beside him, the four brothers silently groomed their mounts with curry combs and hard brushes.

"Seems so," the Deacon said softly.

"Town rises early in this here heat," Doc said over his animal's back.

"Guess so," the man in black mumbled as he rubbed the tiny mites from his horse's ears. The Deacon patted his mount's forehead before leaving the humid stable.

"Real sociable," Samuel said to his animal.

"Right strange, that one is," Doc replied, rubbing his horse's hard shoulder. When Doc stroked his animal's withers, the mount stretched his neck forward and closed his large black eyes. The animal nickered with pleasure.

"Got some burr under his saddle, I'd say," added the youngest brother.

"At least this town has more than one saloon," Doc said to his horse. "No need drinking with the likes of that fellow."

"As good a place as any to spend the three days what's left," Luke said beside his animal.

"Sounds good to me," Jason nodded.

Chapter Twelve

THE LITTLE BRASS TOAD PERCHED on the El Sapo table grinned at the black shoulder of the Deacon. Beneath his freshly brushed hat, the Deacon narrowed his eyes to study the hand of new cards. The nighttime din of the saloon rose on swirls of smoke from dozens of hard faces leaning over gaming tables. In the center of the round table surrounded by eight gamblers and hangers-on, there sat a heavy brass device on a little marble stand for cutting the corners of decks of cards.

Noise, smoke, painted chorus girls, and squinty-eyed men filled the large saloon down the dirt street from the Grand Hotel. The oak bar was as long as the building and thirty patrons tipped their glasses under a huge, wavy mirror.

At another table, a crown and anchor set spilled tokens among the players. Beside the Deacon's table, a finely carved and inlaid Diana table was nearly empty except for five brave souls who challenged the Diana table odds stacked in favor of the house. In the sooty air heavy with evening heat, twenty men laughed at the keno table where the roller spun a wooden goose filled with wooden eggs.

At the Deacon's corner of the rich-man's saloon, the painted ladies hung on men standing near the Deacon.

They studied the Deacon's hand and measured it against the case keeper sitting on the table displaying the cards drawn and played.

When the sour-faced Deacon laid down his hand, four men at the table moaned and laid down their losing cards. Without smiling, the Deacon poured fists of tokens into the deep pockets of his black waistcoat.

"Enough for one night, boys," the Deacon nodded at his winnings.

When the company parted to permit the Deacon to walk toward the cashier, the tallest and most buxom of the women took the big man's arm. At the teller's cage, he emptied his pockets.

"Coin, please," the Deacon ordered. "In two sacks."

"Quite a haul for one night," the painted woman cooed beside the cashier's window.

"Yes, ma'am," the Deacon drawled. He did not turn to face her warm breath close to his lined neck.

"I could turn some of that into a little comfort, if you have a mind for some company." She smiled and her grease paint cracked around her lips.

The Deacon filled his pockets with two sacks of coin which hung beside his two handirons. He turned to study the face panting alcohol vapors into his sweating cheek. Youth had abandoned her flaccid face long before the gambler had ever heard of Cedar City. His mind lingered on the memory of his month of sleeping fitfully on hard earth. He smiled his tight grin.

"Sorry, ma'am. But I have other business."

Brushing past the disappointed working woman, the tall shootist touched the brim of his wide hat in a courtly, parting gesture.

"You here for the rendezvous, ain't you?" Her words

followed the Deacon into the mob of gamers and cigar smoke.

He turned back toward the woman who stood half naked in the oily light. In his hard face, she read his coming and his going.

"Hope they shoot your face off, mister." Her cold words bored like weevils into the tall man's lonesome heart.

They turned their backs to each other at the same instant, she to grab the elbow of the nearest gambler and he to plow through the crowd toward the doorway. Ten paces from the darkness beyond the swinging doors, the Deacon sensed someone eyeing him from two tables away. He looked sideways and found the sweating, stubbled face of a middle-aged man who looked hard toward the Deacon. After a moment, the card-player had to turn away and look down at five empty glasses beside a small pile of coins. The Deacon pushed through the doors into the street.

Behind him, the other gambler emptied a glass and turned to his partner.

"I'm telling you, he's the one. I seen him maybe five years ago at Fort Laramie. Wilson told me about him. Sold his own pard. And Wilson don't lie. He's the one. You ain't likely to forget that face."

"Ah, go on. Five years out here is a long time. All them new Charlies looks the same. Wilson or no, it ain't likely him."

"I'm telling you, now. It were a couple months before the war ended back east. That fellow was in the high country right after Sand Creek. Maybe he even was at Sand Creek. Cheyenne catched him and his pard. Cousins or brothers, maybe. Wilson he says that Black Kettle hisself was there. Gonna skin 'em both alive, he was."

The second man was listening hard now, through the surrounding noise of hard men and easy women.

"That there tall one traded his own kin for his life. Made such a fuss that old Black Kettle wouldn't respect him by killing him. So the Cheyenne let him go free and they kept his pard. Wilson says they tried to skin the other one alive, but he wouldn't die. Dyin' so hard scared them Cheyenne aweful. Let him go, too, after they cut him good. Must have died out in the country some'eres, or got et by wolves. Over twelve years ago. Dead for certain."

Both men looked at the doors as other thirsty men came in.

"Go on and deal, now. I'm telling you it ain't him."

In November 1864, the Third Colorado Cavalry attacked Black Kettle's Cheyenne encampment at Sand Creek. Two Hundred Cheyenne were massacred, mostly women and children. The soldiers butchered the Cheyenne dead, mutilating the bodies. They played catch with severed breasts and cut babies out of their mother's bellies. Dead braves were castrated.

Outside the bawdy saloon, the night air was thick and uncomfortable. A whiff of lilac water rose to the Deacon's nostrils from his perspiring upper lip. Behind where he paused on the wooden sidewalk, the windows cast a shaft of pale light onto the dark street.

The Deacon stepped into the dust. He wore his spurs although he did not need them in town. But he took comfort from their silvery song. The humid air carried sound well and the voices laughing inside the drinking hall followed him into the darkness. He walked behind the few horses tied to hitching rails where musty smelling animals pawed the dry earth. Horses on long reins nuzzled the withers of the animals beside them. In the upper rooms of the saloons along the avenue, hungry men off the Overland did likewise with women who bathed standing up at wash basins until their next customer.

He walked alone and welcomed the solitude of the night. The Deacon did not walk on the wooden sidewalk. When he crossed the corridor of yellow light streaming from one saloon after another, he could see his shadow accompanying him. Among the Indian nations where he had traded and had made medicine in his youth, it was said that a man's death walks beside him at his shoulder. He thought of that when another shaft of light surged from a cheap hotel and his shadow peeked at him. He quickened his pace.

In front of the darkened fortress of the Cattleman's Bank and Trust, the Deacon paused. Standing alone in the dark, he studied the stone front with its thick bars of iron on the windows. Then he moved on toward the Grand Hotel where lights pushed back the darkness all the way to the other side of the street.

In the Grand's brilliant entrance, the Deacon squinted from the bright oil lamps. The cheery main floor buzzed with guests, some in seedy trail clothes and others in their riverboat finest. Laden with his pockets full of coin and two heavy revolvers, the Deacon paid no mind to either the peasants or the princes of railroads and cattle. In his mind he separated the soft pinkness of the barons of capital from the hard-eyed shootists in town by invitation.

"Evening," came a voice at his side.

The Deacon looked into the face of old Doc who nodded at the side of the youngest of the four brothers. Each wore clean clothes and smelled of fatty soap.

"Good evening," the Deacon nodded cordially. He did not smile, but the coldness was gone from his voice.

"Coming in already?" the youth smiled broadly.

"Yes. I'm getting too old to stay out all night. You boys on the make tonight?"

"Doing the town proper," the youth beamed. Doc smiled, too.

"Well, good pickings to both of you."

The two men nodded and headed outside while the Deacon walked to the stairs. Two flights up, he rounded the corner of his floor bathed in pale light from oil lamps along the hallway.

Before he could reach No Account's door, a woman in a long skirt swayed out of the mountain man's room. She paused close to the Deacon who towered above her.

The Deacon looked down into her deer-brown eyes. Her cream paint was smeared around her mouth. From under the grease and sweat, her face still showed the bloom of youth not yet forfeited to her skin trade. The man in black nodded and removed his hat.

"Warm tonight," she sighed as she wiped her forehead with her small, white hand. Auburn curls fell to her shoulders and the tall man forced his eyes away from the damp skin of her neck.

"Yes, miss," the Deacon said softly.

"Would you care for some company, mister?"

The thought of following No Account was gagsome to the tall man whose graying hair just touched his ears.

"Last room on the right," he sighed. "About midnight perhaps."

"Surely," she smiled with perfect teeth. She looked even younger.

The Deacon recovered himself by the time he knocked on the door.

No Account opened his door. The Deacon entered and made for the chair by the open window. He sat down heavily in the little room illuminated by one lamp damped low. In the close air, the room smelled of sweat and perfumed soap.

"Feeling better?" the Deacon asked the little man slouched in the room's other chair.

The man in light cotton drawers smiled a wide grin with many black spaces. His wild beard was slightly trimmed and his gaunt face was nearly clean. The Deacon closed his eyes in the yellow gloom of the stuffy room.

"I went to the Cattleman's this morning. Damn place is a fort." The Deacon did not open his eyes.

No Account leaned forward to catch the tall man's subdued voice.

"Saw the vault, too. It's in the rear with guards like the Iron Brigade." Behind his eyes, the Deacon walked the ghastly fields of Gettysburg. "To get into that vault from the outside would take a hole like the one we exploded under the Yankees at Petersburg in '65." The Deacon showed teeth for a moment while he remembered days of glory but forgot about the starvation and the lice.

"Can we take it?" No Account looked worried.

The Deacon raised an eyebrow without opening his eyes.

"Sure. We'll just have to go through the front door like proper gentlemen."

Chapter Thirteen

"DIDN'T MEAN TO WAKE YOU," the Deacon said softly.

The woman in the rumpled bed stirred and opened her eyes. Her red hair covered the pillow. Beside her, the empty place where the Deacon had slept was still warm. She lay on her back and pulled the sheet up to cover her nakedness.

In the first light of dawn, she could see the Deacon across the room. He sat in the chair by the window. His long arms dangled at his sides and his legs were stretched out in front. His graying hair was matted around his face which had lost its hard lines in the morning twilight. Wearing only his white drawers, the tall shootist was at ease.

"You didn't wake me. . . . What are you doing, anyway? It can't be six o'clock yet."

"Just watching, thanks. Wanted to watch you sleep." The Deacon's face, darkened with gray stubble, creased into a warm and gentle smile.

"You paid for all night," the woman muttered sleepily. She remembered who she was. "You won't get your money's worth sitting in that chair in your woollies."

"All night ticket gives me the works; whatever I want. Ain't that the rules?" So softly did the Deacon speak that she had to cock her ear toward him.

"That's the rule, alright." Her lips moved as she worked her morning tongue around her dry mouth.

"Then that's what I choose to buy: watching a beautiful, young woman sleep in my bed." He paused and looked into her eyes. "Sleeping in my bed and looking safe and protected."

The woman blinked hard to catch the sudden wetness at the corners of her eyes.

"What are you? And why are you here?" She whispered over her two fists that held the sheet to her throat.

"Like everyone else in town: here for the prize." The Deacon spoke toward the open window full of gray morning.

"The damned rendezvous!" Her voice cracked. "Damn you!"

"Forgive me. I didn't mean to wake you. It's hardly light yet."

"It's not that." She was now whimpering, like a child.

"Then what is it?" His words caught in his throat.

With her tearful face turned away from her paying fare, the woman thought about the tall man's hands. Her narrow body had known many hard hands which left blue bruises upon her thighs. But this man's hands, hardened by his grip on leather and on ivory-handled irons, were more gentle than even her first man—a farm boy whose name she could not recall. She could not even remember the boy's face. But the memory of his gently searching hands had remained with her all the years. As the tall stranger waited patiently, the woman thought of the shootist's hands.

"Nothing," she whispered. "Nothing at all."

There was a long silence. The woman closed her eyes. As she dozed, the Deacon lowered his lined face, the better to study the smooth line of her white cheek free of grease paint. As the new sun burned red outside the window two days before the rendezvous, her hair glowed. Her curls took on the color of a high-country campfire which the Deacon's mind could still remember from the dreams of his youth.

"I have to dress," he said softly as he stood. "I have early business. You can stay and sleep." His knees cracked as he pushed out of the deep chair. In the brooding silence, the Deacon washed and shaved over the basin set atop a bureau beside the window.

In full daylight, the woman rolled over to watch the Deacon adjust his gold watch chain across his tight, black vest. Sunlight glinted off his twin handirons low on his black waist.

"Stay as long as you like," he said as he pulled on his black waistcoat. He carried his wide-brimmed hat and stopped at the closed door near the wash basin. He had already put two gold coins next to the water pitcher. She was pay-in-advance. With his hand on the doorknob, the big man searched the woman's eyes. "Thank you, kindly," he whispered as he took long steps into the dark hallway. He closed the door lightly. He did not see the woman bury her good face in the pillow.

The Deacon walked down the hallway. He listened to the music of his heel chains muted by the carpet. When his boots stepped onto the wooden stairs, his spurs jingled manfully. Walking down the staircase, the Deacon smiled the smile of a man not hungry and in no hurry.

Only a few early risers milled about the cheery foyer of the Grand Hotel. The well-dressed peddlers were clear eyed and anxious to hawk their wares. The hard-jawed shootists wore the pursed brows of men gorged on cheap corn liquor.

Advancing from the airy Grand into the street's brilliant morning, the Deacon unconsciously felt for the comforting company of the heavy handirons dangling at his sides under his coat. He adjusted their soothing weight as he walked in the dust toward the stone facade of the Cattleman's Bank and Trust. The weight of the coin in his pockets from the night's gaming tables made his long coat swing across his sides in exaggerated arcs.

The Deacon entered the stone bank. He was surprised to find himself in the midst of a large crowd. As his eyes grew accustomed to the shadows inside, he pulled his gold watch from his vest. It was only eight o'clock and the bank had not been open ten minutes. The ballroom-size foyer with its polished floor and ceiling murals was already filled with noisy customers more appropriate for lunch-hour traffic.

With his eyes adapted to the inside gloom, the Deacon studied two lines of men waiting for a teller's cage. Some were dressed in frayed shirts and tattered dusters right off the Overland. Others were outfitted like the Deacon, as if awaiting a sternwheeler at a Memphis wharf. The Deacon noted that every man in line was packing a shooting iron on his hip. The massive bank was infested with men in town by invitation—all hoping that his morning business would not be his last transaction. Beneath the huge chandelier of lighted oil lamps, the Deacon knew that he stood shoulder to shoulder with his own kind. The thought chilled him.

One by one, each customer finished with the teller's window. On each passing face, darting eyes and hurried glances took the measure of the other hard men congregating from all of the wild places of the West.

The Deacon looked over the heads in line ahead of him. Seeing Mr. Thompson on the far side of the building, the Deacon walked to the other line. In Mr. Thompson's line, the tall shootist waited patiently. His mind catalogued each face whose eyes met his. He did not bother to memorize the eyes that blinked and turned away. Those eyes which did not turn away he committed to memory as firmly as the smell of his mother's kitchen.

"Good morning, Mr. Thompson," the Deacon smiled when his turn came.

The thin teller swallowed. "And to you, sir."

"For your fine fortress," the Deacon said as he laid two heavy bags of coin on the counter between the teller's soft, white hands, which protruded from sleeves held up with black garters.

"Deposit, sir?"

"Please."

"And I am only to remember your face, right?"

"Yes indeed, Mr. Thompson." The Deacon's narrow eyes glanced behind the young teller toward the hidden vault.

"Be making a withdrawal day after tomorrow?" The youth struggled to smile. His smooth face twitched nervously.

"Hope so, Mr. Thompson. But you never can tell."

Mr. Thompson nodded inside his little cage like a condemned man anxiously awaiting his hearty meal.

Taking his leave with a nod, the Deacon elbowed his way toward the door. He noticed an armed guard on each side of the massive doors. Their repeater rifles gleamed blackly in the fierce daylight. More guards armed like cavalry regulars stood outside in the sunshine. When the Deacon looked into one of their faces, the Pinkerton man lowered his eyes, quickly.

In the bright daylight of morning, the Deacon stepped down from the wooden sidewalk's planks into the street filling with townspeople who kept their distance from the heavily armed strangers. He stopped short with his heels touching the sidewalk behind him. He did not turn around. His instincts honed fine by a lifetime living at wits' end made him pause in the sunshine. The hair on the back of his neck bristled.

When a wad of tobacco spit splattered the dry street at the Deacon's boots, the tall man sighed. He did not look up. He did not turn around.

"Marshal," the Deacon said between clenched teeth. He stepped over the black spot on the sandy street.

Hearing nothing, the Deacon walked away.

Chapter Fourteen

THE HART BROTHERS SAT WITH DOC. In the Wednesday afternoon noise of the poor-man's smoky saloon, dozens of dusty men poured sour mash whiskey down parched throats.

In a corner of the rowdy cat house, the four brothers and Doc huddled over a shabby table. Instead of a fine gaming table and the patina of aged wood, the table was dressed in crudely carved names and obscenities. Most of the awkward letters cut into the wood were the only writing known to the men whose only monument in the world was their brand etched in liquor stained pine.

On the rutted table lay set screws, barrel wedges, and blackened cylinders from the handirons of the five men hunched over their dismembered hardware. The oily scent of black powder fouling mingled with the saloon's smoky haze. They rubbed their oiled weapons until the shine came up.

"Won't be long now," the middle brother mumbled to his pile of iron. His voice searched for reassurance.

"Friday," Jason said into the six-chambered cylinder close to his squinting eye. He aimed the round cylinder of his handiron toward the wavy glass of the saloon's window. The oldest brother could see yellow daylight in the tiny hole of each chamber's "nipple" end, tapered to hold the ignition percussion cap.

"Guess we've come quite a piece," added the cheerful, red-bearded face of Luke.

"Wonder what it'll be like with all them shooters blasting away across the countryside?" Samuel, the middle brother, addressed the cylinder impaled on his little finger which emerged covered with black fouling.

"Be like?" Doc said working his gnarled hands over his oiled hardware. "Be like hell come out of the ground."

Each of the five men sat under his sweat-stained hat. Frank sported his Montana peak. The rest of the rabble ignored the five men at the table.

"What's your plan, Brother?" the youngest asked Jason whose gray beard showed traces of powder fouling.

Jason laid his iron on the table. He leaned back in his chair.

"Same as always: We stick together . . . the five of us." He glanced sideways at Doc. "We cover each other. Always worked before."

Jason looked to Doc.

"Proud to ride with you boys," Doc grinned to his only real family. "Friday, and after."

"The shoot," Jason continued, "will be a real free-for-all. We best stick close." He looked into each anxious face, one by one.

The other men nodded. They worked silently at their weapons.

"Still thinking about that bottom land?" Luke asked Jason.

"Yep. A few hundred acres of the best. What about you when we collect our share of the gold?"

The big man with the red beard snapped the barrel

wedge into his weapon to hold the pieces together.

Jason nodded and raised his glass to seal a bargain between brothers.

"Would you mind a neighbor?" Luke smiled.

"How you boys fixed?" said a voice through the dense smoke and noise. The five men looked up at a heavyset and sweating bargirl.

"Could use another round for all, thanks," Samuel answered.

"All around," she smiled. "Quite a pile of hardware." She scanned the old handirons.

"All ball and cap?" She sounded surprised. "Most of these Charlies have them new Peacemakers. Not many bother anymore with caps and powder flasks." As she waddled toward the bar, the sitting men heard her mumble "Poor dumb bastards."

For a moment, the five men looked down at their antique handirons.

"I don't know," Jason said thoughtfully as he cradled his old Remington in his hands. "Sure has been with me a long time. Since before the war. Sometimes, old and trusty is best." He looked around the table and he welcomed the four nods of assent.

Returning with a dirty pitcher of warm beer, the woman smiled at the little company of dusty men.

"On the house, boys. . . . On me," she smiled warmly.

Jason poured the brew into five greasy glasses. He lifted his glass which caught the yellow lamplight.

"To us poor, dumb bastards!" the oldest brother grinned broadly.

"Poor bastards," the four other men repeated and quickly downed the frothy ale. Then they pushed back from the table.

Jason fumbled with his handiron and he gave the shiny cylinder a final spin at half-cock. The troop around him did likewise.

Putting iron to leather, the five men waded out of the sea of stale smoke and into the daylight outside. They passed sweating men who cussed and drank their fear away. The saloon was full of men whose courage came from knowing that they had nowhere better to be. To hearty men who carry their world wrapped inside a single bedroll, one place is as good as another for testing and winning, or for testing and dying.

The cool evening air was a welcome comfort after the stifling heat of the loud saloon. The sky was turning twilight gray in the east and red low in the west.

The five men ambled lazily toward the livery to pay the day's visit to their animals which would be needed in two days. They brushed and watered their trusted mounts and whispered into furry, pointed ears.

By the time the five men left the stable for their rooms, the sky was growing dark. The townfolk had long since locked their shutters to keep out the wilderness and the hungry gunmen from across the land. Without looking up, the five men walked under the banner hanging limply from the livery: "WELCOME ASSASSINS AND ROAD SCUM."

They walked in the gloom past the Cattleman's Bank. The half doors of several saloons leaked light upon the street. They could hear the hard banter of men drinking, gaming, and buying flesh.

One block from the Grand Hotel, they passed the Sheriff's Office. Oil lamps burned in the barred windows. The five men could not hear the talk from inside the jailhouse. They did not pause to listen. Their minds were of one thought: A man deserves a hot shave and an all-night woman before he rides head high and heels down into eternity.

Frank led the way toward Comfort Alley. The late-night street was crowded. All the men going one way aimed for the row of saloons and all the men walking in the opposite direction with the brothers and Doc headed for soft skin and dirty linens.

"HEARD YOU WAS among 'em, Marshal. Glad you dropped by." The Cedar City sheriff sat behind his cluttered desk in the jailhouse. His dirty boots at the ends of his long legs were propped atop his desk. He toyed with his thick, handlebar mustache. "Good to see you, old friend."

"Thanks," the retired marshal smiled as he fired a direct hit into the spittoon on the floor. He slouched in his chair which creaked backwards. The big man's boots also rested on the sheriff's desk.

"Didn't figure you would be among this rabble trickling off the Overland from every cat house west of Saint Louis."

"Didn't plan it this way," the marshal spat. "Just happened." The rumpled lawman sighed.

"Not too late, you know, to lay low Friday. You and I have surely had a lifetime of near misses. Seems something of a pity to cash in now. Odds ain't exactly with someone your age anyhow." The town sheriff took a deep drag on his pipe which sent clouds of sweet smoke toward the ceiling. His face behind the smoke was browned and leathery. Furrows cut his face into stubbled sections and deep crow's feet cracked around his eyes. The hair at his temples was well grayed.

"Maybe, Sheriff," the marshal nodded as he turned the tobacco chaw over in his mouth. "It does seem a long ride down here, over a month, just to stay in bed on rendezvous day." Splat! Another shot hit the spittoon. The tail of the wad trickled down the lawman's cheek onto his stained shirt.

The sheriff puffed his curved pipe and enjoyed the company of his friend.

"Sounds like you're not too sure where you'll make your stand, Marshal. Any idea?"

"Well, I wouldn't be surprised to see a little goings-on right here in town. There is a king's ransom over at the Cattleman's, you know."

"I know," the sheriff nodded inside a cloud of smoke. "What about you?"

"I'll start things off afield. Don't want no shooting near town. The city fathers already want my hide hanging out to dry for putting out the invite to all them assassins. . . . Expect trouble at the bank, do you?"

"Think maybe," the marshal nodded with a brown drool.

"But the Cattleman's guarded like Mr. Lincoln's tomb! No one going to get around them guards. Only a damned fool would try." The sheriff smiled knowingly as if he had all of his angles covered.

"Only a damned fool," the former lawman spat.

"No, sir. Don't think anyone would set his sights on the Cattleman's." The sheriff sent a blue smoke ring over the head of his guest.

"Tell me, what in heaven's name possessed you to conjure up this whole shooting party? Never did hear of any such thing."

"Well," the sheriff said thoughtfully, "I'll be retiring soon. Wanted to clean up this territory before I move out to pasture. Couldn't go after all of them man-killers and wife-stealers out there. So," he took a long drag on the old pipe, "so, I just invited all of 'em right down here. Let 'em all blow theirselves away for me. Every town and bank in the territory put up part of the gold bounty to attract the worst of 'em." The lawman smiled at his own smarts. "The last ones standing should get a damned medal, along with their share of the prize."

"So you be serious about handing the gold over to the survivors?" Spit; drool.

"Serious as death and taxes. They only came on account of my word being good."

"Never heard nothing like it." The older man shook his sweating head.

"Me neither. . . . Them boys what rode in with you, you riding with them?"

"Oh, we rode the Overland together. Not a bad lot, them brothers. But the other two—the dandy and the trapper—they bear watching." A hard look came over the marshal's face.

"The one looking like a parson and the one what stinks: They together?"

"Don't know. But I have a bad feeling about them. Ain't seen them together really." The thick man wiped brown sweat from around his mouth.

"Well," the sheriff grinned through a blast of smoke. "Friday should tell." The sheriff tapped his pipe out on the desk top. "You don't wear the badge no more?"

"No," the thick man spat. He looked behind the sheriff at the row of iron cages where half a dozen drunks snored restlessly on urine-soaked cots. "Seen enough jailhouses and hanging trees for one lifetime."

The marshal stood in the humid cloud of smoke that looked yellow in the oily light from the lantern on the desk. The dusty visitor stopped at the open doorway. The lamp lit only half of his grizzled face.

"Take care," the visitor smiled.

"And you, old friend."

Stepping into the darkness of the street, the old law-man followed a trail of footprints to the Grand and its brilliant lights.

The marshal's spurs jingled their familiar song, muted by the carpet, as he climbed the staircase. He walked slowly on legs still sore from the long trail.

IN THE LAST of twilight, the dust of Comfort Alley seemed to hang in the air. Having soldiered, Jason Hart thought he saw enough men to muster a regiment.

Comfort Alley was more a bivouac than a street. There were no real buildings, except for the outhouses. The alley was a ribbon of dirt street between two rows of canvas tents erected just outside the Cedar City village. The tents were large, like the field hospital tents Jason remembered after Sharpsburg and Bloody Angle at Spotsylvania. Where a tent flap was pulled open, lantern light illuminated little squares of the street and its piles of manure.

If a tent flap were closed, its entrance was guarded by one or two, large and hairy men. If a flap were open, all manner of women stood making easy conversation with the men shopping in the alley. Tall women and short ones, thin or round, white ones or black, or an isolated Indian all talked business with the lonesome men.

"What a menu," Doc grinned cheerfully.

"Ain't you too old," Samuel smiled.

"You see any dirt and daisies on my face, boy?"

"No offense meant, Doc," the middle brother said meekly.

Doc slapped him hard on the back.

"None taken, Samuel." Doc eyed the four brothers. "Don't wait up for me, boys."

When Doc swaggered into the throng, he reached into his duster and pulled out a handful of coins, which he counted in the dark as he walked.

"Like the old man said," Jason grinned as he led his brothers down the temporary road.

They stopped when Frank stopped to study a tent with closed flap. Four tents in a row had a rope cordon around them to do business as a group. Three of the tents had signs reading simply "2$." Each had a door-keeper. Behind the tall man standing sentry at the fourth tent, the sign in crude letters painted on the tent said "2$ OR BATH AND ALL NIGHT: $20 GOLD."

Frank took off his still crisp, Montana peak and ran his fingers through his greasy hair.

"I think a tub and all night is for me."

"Don't fall in, little brother," Luke chuckled as he led the other brothers further down the camp ground.

Frank stood awkwardly for fifteen minutes, watching the big man who tended the entrance. They made no small talk. Finally, the tent opened and a cheerful little man walked briskly into the darkness toward a nearby saloon.

"Fast or all-night, boy?" the hawker asked wearily.

"The works."

"Twenty, gold, young fellow," the big man said. Frank flipped him a shiny coin. The man held the flap open and Frank stepped inside.

Frank was met by a small woman wrapped in a long blanket. Her fair hair was short and she looked tired. Lamp light reflecting in her blue-gray eyes made Frank forget to breathe.

He studied her closely. She saw the recognition in his eyes.

"You're with the brothers, aren't you?"

"Yes, ma'am. I'm sorry. But I'm surprised, is all." He was stammering, which made him look even younger. "I rode next to you damn near a month. I thought you was a boy."

"No," Marybeth Hutchinson said, opening her blanket around her naked body and closing it again when the tent flap opened. The big man from outside struggled in with a large wooden bucket of steaming water in each hand. He poured the hot water into a horse trough already half full of dirty water from her last all-night customer.

"You be all night, then?"

"Yes, ma'am."

"Then get in the tub before it cools off."

Frank hesitated. He suddenly felt very foolish, like everyone outside would be listening to him.

The prostitute shuffled to the single lamp atop a cracker box set on end. She lowered the wick until only gray shadows covered the canvas walls. Frank slowed when he stripped down to his woollies. She saw his eyes glint near the oil lamp.

"I seen it before," the woman said without a smile on her sweating face.

* * *

WELL AFTER MIDNIGHT, the Deacon walked up the main street toward the Grand. Loud men still milled about, tramping hard paths in the dirt street between the saloons and the whores' tents.

Coming up to the jet-black night between two deserted buildings, the Deacon heard No Account's voice. The voice was pleading.

"T'ain't so! T'ain't so!"

"Hard as a hooker's heart! Your brains is as hard as a hooker's heart!" Youthful voices were singing the words over and over, like a chant.

Five boys turned around from No Account when the light from a saloon across the street went out suddenly. They turned to see the Deacon filling the narrow space between the buildings.

"Move on, boys."

No Account retreated further into a dark cranny in the alley. The boys said nothing.

The Deacon reached into his pockets and pulled out small change. He tossed the coins toward the feet of the closest tormentor. The dirty-faced boy, hardly out of his teens, stooped down and scooped up coins and sand.

"Take your friends down the way and get some mud for your little turtles."

When the Deacon stepped sideways, the wide-eyed boys ran past him in terrified single-file.

No Account stepped into the gray shadow cast by the lights in the windows across the street. The Deacon closed the distance between them.

A fine trickle of blood oozed from one of the ragged man's nostrils. His eyepatch was flipped up onto his

sweating forehead, revealing an empty socket surrounded with dark crust.

The Deacon took off his wide hat and pushed it under
his arm, taking care not to crush it. No Account's good
eye was still wide with anger and fear. Without a word,
the tall man reached over and set the eyepatch back into
position. Then he pulled a white handkerchief from his
vest pocket, spit on it, and wiped the blood from No
Account's face. The Deacon was as gentle as a mother.

Chapter Fifteen

FRANK HART AWOKE SLOWLY WHEN someone touched his shoulder. Opening his eyes, he saw his all-night woman standing beside the cot that they had shared for twenty dollars gold. She was dressed in a long rumpled skirt with a faded floral design. It looked like parchment in the morning sunlight filtering through the canvas tent.

"Time for you to go, Frank."

When he sat up, a sweat-soaked blanket fell away from his bare chest. Frank looked down sleepily and then up at the woman. Even with the dark circles under her hauntingly blue eyes, she looked like a schoolgirl with the strained sunlight through the canvas shining on her face. Her short hair was uncombed and looked chopped by a blind barber. When Frank hesitated to climb out of bed, the woman smiled for a heart beat before a peculiar hardness returned to her face. The hollows of her pale cheeks made her look hungry since birth.

"I'll wait outside while you get dressed, Frank."

"Thanks, ma'am."

Marybeth stepped outside into the brilliant morning where coffee steamed near dozens of little firepits crackling between the tents. Inside, Frank dressed quickly, putting on his union suit and light shirt, both of which smelled like three days in wilting heat. When he rinsed his mouth from a pitcher of warm water set on the dirt floor, he spit into the full bath trough. He had to smile that the customer who preceded his bath had probably done the same.

The sun low over the craggy ridges east of Cedar City was blinding when Frank stepped into Thursday morning. He pulled his hat low over his painful eyes. Standing beside the woman who had given him her comfort, he could not find words. She was not his first by-the-hour woman; but she was the first who did not seem to know much about her craft.

"I guess I'll be doing breakfast now, ma'am."

"Yes. Well, good luck tomorrow."

He nodded. Frank needed a pile of hot griddle cakes and coffee as badly as he had needed the bath and the poke. While he looked down at Marybeth, over her shoulder he saw last night's money-taker approaching from Main Street's row of saloons that did not seem to close.

"Everything alright here?" the big man asked with a chilly voice.

"Fine," Marybeth said.

"The old lady was disappointed that you only gave five rides last night."

"But this one was twenty dollars." Marybeth looked neither hurt nor angry. She was simply talking business.

"I told her that."

Marybeth shrugged and Frank felt uneasy.

"Well, like I said, I need to go over to the Widow Maker for some breakfast. Maybe another time, Marybeth."

"Sure." She turned back toward the big man with hair to his broad shoulders.

"I'm just telling you what the old lady said. She said you was giving it away at the Grand. That mule-skinner Charlie. I'm just telling you."

Frank touched the corner of his hat when the small woman glanced up at him. Her expression made his boots stop. He instantly remembered the same eyes, only black, on the face of a foal tangled in barbed wire.

"Good-bye, Frank."

"Ma'am." When she blinked and looked away, the youngest Hart brother walked on. He could not look back.

Another scraggly drifter walked past Frank before he had gone ten paces. He heard the man's voice behind him.

"How much for an hour?"

"Two dollars." The voice was the big man who carried messages from the woman who ran the four tents roped off from the rest where women worked alone.

"I'm tired," Marybeth said softly. "Go next door. You'll have a good time there."

"I like little 'ns, like you, missy."

"Two dollars," the big man said.

Frank turned around. He did not know what to do when he saw Marybeth standing between her keeper and the customer whose twin Peacemakers protruded from his duster which reached his spurs. Two dollars in gold passed in front of the woman who looked up toward Frank ten yards away.

With the glaring sun shoulder high to his left, Frank clearly saw her eyes glistening.

The ruffian grabbed her by the wrist and dragged her into the tent.

"You'll do as you're told! Two dollars worth!" The loud voice carried through the closed tent flap. The door-keeper stood dumbly in the sunshine.

"What's the riot?" a woman's cold voice called.

Frank saw a middle-aged woman walking from the tent two spaces over, still within the roped-off compound.

"Marybeth don't want to work."

"Oh, we'll just see." The round woman threw the canvas flap aside and marched into the tent. The thin air made her shrill voice sound far off to Frank who could not move.

"I took you in when you had no place to go and no money. I've paid you fair wages for three days. If this gentleman wants your services, he'll get them, by God. Now you do as you're told."

The sounds of ripping clothing and shouting women erupted inside the large tent. Other men and other painted women, some in their underwear, slowly gathered between Frank and the big man standing guard. Hard laughter could be heard from inside, above the chatter of twenty people who quickly assembled to listen.

"Ungrateful bitch!" the older woman's voice screamed. "That's how you come into this God-forsaken world, by God, and that's how the likes of you will go out!"

The tent stakes climbed three inches out of the hard dirt when Marybeth Hutchinson rolled through the tent flap and flipped over one of the ropes taught between the ground and the canvas corner.

The girl was stark naked when she crumbled to the dust. In the sunshine, her body was as white as the gypsum earth. She fell into a pale ball, crouching to conceal herself from the hooting and laughing gawkers. She bent forward to hide her breasts until her forehead touched the street close to a fresh horse pie.

Without thinking, Frank pushed hard through the growing crowd. He took off his duster and threw it over the hysterical girl as if he were smothering a fire.

Blinking in a cloud of talcum-fine dust, he looked up as the woman and man came out of the tent. Both were laughing.

The man stepped quickly toward Frank and gently pushed his shoulder where he squatted beside Marybeth. Her face dropped tears onto Frank's dirty boots.

"You had your ride, mister. She's mine now till seven o'clock."

The man was still laughing when his right hand fell to his revolver stock inside his duster. His fingers were open wide and away from the trigger guard.

"Just back off easy," Frank said softly through clenched teeth. "Be plenty of shooting tomorrow. No need to start today."

Frank stood up, leaving the girl weeping with her head covered by the long duster. Her bare dirty feet and white ankles stuck out in the sunshine.

"She ain't working now," Frank said as calmly as he could. The crowd moved back in lock-step. He slowly reached into his left pocket and pulled out two dollars. He threw the coins into the dust beside Marybeth. His right hand went down slowly beside his holster.

The suddenly grim customer squinted.

"There's your two dollars, friend. Take it next door and party there."

"Cain't do that, boy."

Without blinking, the man in the trail duster pulled his Peacemaker.

Frank cleared his old cap-and-ball Remington in a blure of blued iron. It exploded so close above the sniffling girl that she yelped when red-hot embers of black powder fell on the backs of her legs.

The stunned stranger fired one round into the street beside his boot as his toes lifted up and he tumbled backwards, spinning over the same tent rope that had drawn blood across the naked girl's thighs. He took his last breath on his back as his spurs spun in the air where the rope had caught him behind the knees.

When Frank looked at the crowd, he measured everyone's eyes. His shootist's instincts told him that he could put his handiron back on his hip. Even the big man standing next to the woman who ran the flesh farm stepped backward and raised both of his palms toward Frank.

"Take it somewhere else, mister," the angry woman shouted. "Take the little whore with you." The woman's mean eyes did not look down at either the dead customer or the prostrate girl. "She ain't hardly green-broke to ride, anyway." She turned to the crowd. "My girls is all one-hour-for-one-dollar for first takers."

The crowd dissolved in a cloud of dust and laughing women.

Frank helped Marybeth to her feet. Her face was smudged with brown where her tears had turned the street into salty mud.

"Come on, now. Come on, Marybeth."

Frank steadied her and buttoned the duster around her waist. He led her whimpering toward Cedar City beyond the tent city of prostitutes. Men who had not used their given names for years made room on the wooden sidewalk for the young shootist escorting a barefoot woman. Her hair was so short that some of them thought Frank was holding up a drunken boy.

"What the hell happened down there?"

Frank saw the Cedar City sheriff come straight at him. The lawman was half-dressed with his trouser suspenders running across the tops of his long woollies. He had not put on his shirt, but he did wear his six-gun. His emaciated deputy stood sleepily at his side.

"Now you just stop right there, both of you."

Frank and Marybeth stopped.

The sheriff looked closely at Marybeth. She was still buttoning up Frank's duster. Her feet and bare arms coming out of the sleeves near her throat told him what he needed to know.

"A woman? An alley whore? What's going on? Where the hell are your clothes? This used to be a clean damn town! It's hardly six o'clock."

"There's a dead man back there at the tents. I killed him. He laid hands on the girl."

"Laid hands?" The sheriff was deadly serious and puzzled. "Did he pay for her?"

"Yes, but . . ."

"Then business is business, boy. You say you killed him?"

Marybeth looked up at Frank who released his grip on her shoulders.

"I did. He laid hands on the girl without her say-so."

"You said he paid, boy. Rights is rights. At least until tomorrow. You better come with me."

"My brothers is at the Grand. What about the girl?"

The sheriff eyed Marybeth and stroked his stubbled shin. His fresh whiskers were gray like his thinning hair. He had not taken time to put on his hat.

"I'll take her home."

Frank raised an eyebrow.

"To my wife, boy. Trust me." The sheriff looked Frank hard in the eye. Had the shootist not trusted the sheriff, he would not have come to this town.

"Alright, Sheriff. Could you get her some shoes? The street must be like a frying pan already."

"Yes, yes. What's your name, girl?"

"Marybeth," Frank answered.

"Alright, Marybeth. Both of you come with me. I'll send my deputy to fetch your brothers. What's your name, boy?"

"Frank. Frank Hart."

"The Hart Brothers? I should have know'd. You rode in with the marshal, the old man, and them others. Let's go. Harley, you go on down to the alley first."

The deputy jogged toward the busy tents.

With the sheriff walking behind Frank and Marybeth who walked with their arms touching, no one on the busy street paid any attention. If anyone even noticed that one of the three was barefoot, no one paused to look. On the last day before the rendezvous, locals had been boarding up their store fronts since dawn and the strangers were already making smoke in saloons or going for rides in the tents.

"Here," the sheriff said behind the pair who stopped at the jailhouse. Marybeth hesitated. "You'll be safe, missy. Go on in."

He had to push the girl through the doorway. Inside, she found a corner where she stood looking down at the plank floor. The sheriff took Frank's gun belt. The girl could not lift her face to watch Frank step into a cell where the iron door closed behind him. She had seen it all before. Two of last night's rowdy drunkards did not stir when Frank sat down on the last available cot. Half a dozen other men stood silently with their wrists dangling through the bars of a row of cages. All of their eyes focused on the white feet of the woman lost inside the oversized trail duster. A day or two of grime and sweat made their faces shine like they had bathed in oil.

"Do you have anything to say for yourself before I walk the woman home?"

Frank shrugged and looked up at the lawman.

"That other man went for his handiron. Everyone saw it. I done him before he could do me—or her." Frank nodded toward Marybeth who had scrunched down just enough to cover her toes with the duster. She bowed her head, trying to hide her face from the rough men who eyed her with hunger. The duster could not conceal that she was a woman, inspite of her dirty face and mangy hair.

"Probably, boy. They's all the same in the alley. You among 'em. One less trail tramp to bleach in the desert tomorrow, I suppose. But you just cool your heels in there. I still have a town to run and the people what elected me for the last twenty years expect me to lock you up. But you won't have to wait for no judge."

Frank imaged a sudden tightness in his neck. His face hardened.

"Don't worry, boy. I'll turn all of your kind loose come morning. God can judge you just fine at the shoot."

The youngest of the brothers did not feel comforted.

"Marybeth, you come with me. And you boys just stay quiet. My deputy will be back after he cleans up the mess this one made out back."

The sheriff opened the door and the girl stepped into the blinding sun still low in the east. She stepped lightly on the splinters of the rough and hot sidewalk.

"Don't forget shoes, Sheriff," a voice called at the officer's back. He closed the door without a word.

Crossing the wide street, Marybeth walked with her eyes cast down lest she trip barefoot over a fresh horse pie. On the opposite sidewalk, the pair were stopped by a group of ragged boys led by a dour old man.

"Mr. Palmer," the sheriff nodded.

"On my way to the alley, Micah. Heard about the shooting. Good practice for these boys, it is." The white-haired man smiled cheerfully.

"Suppose so," the sheriff said dryly. "Don't teach them boys anything else down there."

Seven boys, barely teenagers, laughed nervously behind the town's undertaker. He had hired a dozen youthful assistants at a penny a day for the rendezvous. For a week, they practiced embalming every barnyard animal that succumbed to worms or disease. With the wind at the boys' tattered backs, the sheriff could smell alcohol in his sweating nostrils.

"Good day, Micah. Come, boys." The frail-looking embalmer led his wards like a mother duck.

"Oh, Mr. Palmer: When Harley is done down there, better remind him to fetch the Hart Brothers from the Grand. I'm holding their kin at the jail. If they ain't at the hotel, tell him to try the Widow Maker."

The undertaker waved over his shoulder toward the backs of Marybeth and the sheriff who turned a corner to a dirt street lined on both sides with rundown houses. Boxes for flowers hung beneath a few of the wavy windows. The coarse planters looked filled with tinder in the overpowering heat.

The sheriff swung open a gate and Marybeth led the way up a walk of hot flagstones. When the sheriff's spurs jingled on the front stoop, a round and silver-haired woman opened the door which creaked on rusty hinges.

"Look what I found, Mother," the lawman smiled. "She be as naked as a jay bird under this here coat."

"Mercy, child!" the older woman said with some warmth in her voice. She cast a squinty look toward her husband.

"I ain't peeked, Mother."

"Have some coffee, child, while I find a frock for you and some shoes."

"Yes'm." The girl still clutched Frank's duster tightly to her throat.

"What happened to your hair?" the wife asked gently while she poured.

"I cut it."

"Oh."

"Mother, I have to get back to the jailhouse." He faced the girl. "You can stay with us for a day or two, just till the action is over tomorrow. We'll decide what to do with you then."

"Will Frank be alright? He's a good boy, Sheriff. Not like all them others in town."

"Maybe; maybe not. But he'll be well took care of. Till tomorrow, leastwise."

"Be careful, Father," the red-cheeked woman said, resting her large hands on her hips.

"Yes, Mother."

The sheriff closed the door behind him and he returned to the bright morning.

"What's your name, child?"

The girl paused for a long moment before she looked up from her tin coffee cup which she held in both of her dirty hands. Her nails were ragged and had black semi-circles at their tips. The older woman had to blink when the girl's strangely pale eyes looked closely at her.

"Marybeth Hutchinson. I came down the Overland on Monday."

The woman with the flushed face narrowed her brown eyes.

"Who ain't?"

"If Frank says it was a fair shoot, then it's so."

"Take a load off, boys," the sheriff said with no rancor in his voice. "Sorry the coffee's cold. Too hot even in the morning to fire up the stove. But you're welcome to a cold cup till my deputy gets back."

Only the retired marshal took up a cold tin cup of black coffee. All the prisoners except Frank had retired quietly to the rear of their cells when the three brothers and the marshal entered a few minutes after the sheriff returned. The embalmer had told the deputy bent over the body about the Hart Brothers. When the hard-faced madame passed the word down the line of tents, three grumbling brothers soon arrived tucking in their shirts. They stopped to get the marshal at the Grand on their way to the jail. The old man spoke law and the brothers needed him.

When the brothers entered the jail, the prisoners not too drunk to stand recognized Jason Hart. He was celebrated for his eye and his courage among the hard men who made their living the same way. Prudence inspired the prisoners to back away from the three Hart guns.

When the sheriff asked the brothers to check their hardware at the doorway, they did so without protest. "Cap and ball?" the sheriff said with surprise. "Figured you boys for cartridges." The marshal with the bright shape of a star on the breast of his faded shirt had already vouched for the brothers. That put the town sheriff at ease.

"We ain't no cold-blooded killers," Samuel mumbled toward the sheriff who still wore his braces over his underwear.

"I know what you are. We'll just wait on Harley."

A dozen perspiring faces turned toward the door when the deputy shuffled in from the street. He hung his threadbare hat on a wooden peg jutting from the coarse wall.

"Ain't them supposed to be locked up, too?"

"Ain't done nothing, Harley. They's the Hart Brothers. You know Marshal here."

The deputy rested his right hand on the stock of his holstered revolver, a well worn .38 caliber, Remington five-shot Police Revolver. It looked small under his hand.

"You can ease up on the pea shooter, Harley. These boys ain't packing."

"Oh."

"Make your report, Harley." The sheriff was impatient as he felt the jailhouse running out of oxygen. The door was closed and only small barred windows in the cellblock ventilated the building.

"Well, Sheriff, all the whores said that the dead fella drawed first. He roughed up one of the girls something aweful. Stripped her, he did."

"Yes, yes, Harley. I know. I took the girl home to Emma."

"And the boy there gave him his money and told him to move on. Then the dead fella went for his piece."

"It's just like I told you, Sheriff," Frank said anxiously. "He drew on me."

"So much for a poke and a bath," Jason sighed. He was not yet awake, having been roused from a dead sleep on top of a German girl who spoke no English.

"Jason, the whore I done last night—she's the boy who rode in with that mountain man on the trail!"

All three brothers outside the cages looked stricken.

"A boy?" Luke asked for his brothers.

"No! Damn it all to hell, Luke. He's a woman. A girl. Cut her hair off. Rode beside her for a damned month and didn't know!"

"Lucky for her," Samuel had to smile. He wiped his wet forehead with the back of his hand.

The marshal who was allowed to wear his Peacemaker laid down his empty tin cup. He spoke toward Frank, but his face had a strange expression.

"A girl dressed as a man? Guess I never really got a clear look at her. The way she kept to herself under that hat or stayed close to that mule-skinner."

"Not much to look at," Frank said softly as he sat on his bunk. He leaned backward until he touched the stone wall covered with carved names, initials, and obscene etchings. "But she sure got eyes. Blue like I never did see. Blue as Texas Mountain Laurel. That road scum had no call to thump on her like he done."

The marshal swallowed, blinked and looked down at the floor. Then he stepped away from the huddle of sweaty men.

"Thank you, Harley. Is Mr. Palmer and his boys cleaning up the mess?"

"Yes, Sheriff. They gonna practice, he says, for tomorrow."

"Alright, boys. Pick up your pieces and go on about your business."

"What about Frank?"

"You go on. Pick him up tomorrow at first light. I'll feed him."

The sheriff spoke to Jason who looked over the lawman's shoulder toward his brother in the cage.

"I'll be fine, Jason. Really. Besides, I already spent my last twenty dollars." Frank smiled.

Jason nodded and forced a grin.

"Till tomorrow, Sheriff."

"Tomorrow, Mr. Hart."

Only when Harley opened the thick wooden door did everyone realize that the marshal had already quietly left the jail.

THE DEACON ATE breakfast alone and walked back toward the Grand at 8:30. He did not glance sideways at the town's largest bank. A line of dusty men reached from the Cattleman's foyer into the street as shootists withdrew whatever money they had not gambled away. They needed their cash for one last walk down Comfort Alley or one last hand at the Widow Maker before the rendezvous.

When the Deacon climbed the stairs to his room, he looked down each side of the hallway before he knocked on No Account's door. When the door opened an inch, the Deacon nodded and the door opened wide. He closed it behind him.

"How's your face?"

"Better, Deacon."

"Good. You eat?"

"Yep."

"You understand the plan for tomorrow?"

No Account nodded.

"You need some coin for the day?"

"I ain't going out."

The Deacon looked closely at No Account's face. His beard was trimmed some and his face was washed. He had used a hard bristle brush to curry the grit and dust out of his buckskin shirt.

"You expecting company?" The tall man in black vest suppressed a smile.

"Maybe."

"Try not to catch no drips."

No Account licked his finger tips and pushed his bushy sideburns against his ears.

"Deacon, I aim to plug that old lawman what rode in with us."

"What? Don't be silly. I'll handle him if he gets in the way. If he don't, we'll let him be. Don't need no extra trouble. Just forget it."

No Account walked toward the open window and moved the curtain aside. He looked down into the bustling street.

"It won't be no trouble."

"What's got into you, anyway?" The Deacon was losing patience.

"Nothing."

"Well, then, keep out of trouble today. We have work to do in the morning."

When No Account did not turn away from the window, the Deacon opened the door a crack and looked down the hall. Seeing no one, he leaned forward and looked out in the opposite direction. After a moment, he left the stuffy room for his own.

No Account stayed close to the window all day.

* * *

"THERE'S A MARSHAL in the kitchen to see you, Marybeth. Says he's retired. Micah mentioned him to me yesterday. You'll be alright."

The girl stood in a bright dress. Mid-morning sunlight streaming through the window highlighted the gold in her short hair. It was parted in the middle looking freshly washed. Even her fingernails were clean.

"Well, go on now, girl. I don't want him tracking dust onto my floor all day waiting for you."

Marybeth shuffled toward the tiny kitchen. There was no surprise in her narrowed eyes when she faced the lawman.

"So it is you, Marybeth. I can't believe I didn't see it."

"You shot my man."

To the marshal's ears, her voice sounded as hard as a handful of penny nails inside a tin pail.

"I didn't shoot Saguaro. He done himself. With your little iron."

"That ain't true! And if it was, you would have arrested me back home."

"I didn't arrest you, Marybeth"—he looked down at her sunken and wind-burned cheeks criss-crossed with scratches from a dead rowdy who bought her for two dollars— "because I didn't want you to end up here."

"I don't believe you." She turned her brightly colored back to him. "You killed Saguaro. And if you hadn't, then you would have hung him."

"I would have done that." He had to nod, hat-in-hand. "After tomorrow, I'll take you home to your daddy. He won't know what you done here, down in the alley."

She lowered her face. In a moment, the lawman saw tears dripping beside her too-big shoes.

"I been done over, Marshal. On the trail. Before the alley."

"I'm sorry, Marybeth. You shouldn't have come after me. Don't know what you expected. Jesus. You're just a girl."

"Not any more," she said to the wet floor.

"I'll take you home."

"I'll die first. Like Saguaro."

The marshal had enough. He sighed deeply and pressed his hat to his white hair. The sheriff's wife came into the little room and laid her hand on the weeping girl's shoulder. The old woman looked hard at him. Marybeth Hutchinson did not turn around.

"Then I'll still take you home over my saddle. At least your daddy and that boy sitting down at the jail-house can lay flowers on you."

He looked at the sheriff's red-faced wife.

"Ma'am. Marybeth."

The marshal walked quickly back to the Grand. Even though it was not yet noon, he felt exhausted.

He climbed the hotel stairs slowly. His old legs were still raw from his month in the saddle. At the top of the steps, he nearly bumped into the fleshy woman he had taken on his first night in town.

"Good afternoon, ma'am," he smiled as he removed his dusty hat.

The little woman with pancake powder on her face looked up at him. She studied his sadly peaceful eyes.

"Good-bye, Marshal."

Chapter Sixteen

FIVE DUSTY MILES WEST OF Cedar City, a multitude of mounted men faced the towering rock looming above them. A warm dawn wind blew dryly across the Iron Mountains where the riders reined in their restless animals. The new Friday sky glowed pale blue. When the sky was still dark, the sheriff had opened his jail. Frank joined his brothers. The rest of the prisoners crept home or straight to Comfort Alley to make themselves small and invisible.

Some of the gunmen stood beside their horses. Most nervously took to saddle. Hands not gripping taught reins rested on shooting irons. All of the squinting eyes looked up at the Cedar City sheriff who stood atop the rocks. From the precipice, he looked down upon an army of red-eyed killers. The sheriff's words rang out over the snorting and pawing of the sweating horses.

"Gentlemen: Welcome to the Cedar City Rendezvous. You are all here by invitation and because you know that my word is as good as the gold yonder at the Cattleman's."

The thin, hot air carried the sheriff's words. He did not have to shout since all ears were cocked toward him.

"There be five miles 'tween here and town. The object is for you to get from here to there . . . alive enough to claim the prize gold. Those of you what make it that far will get an equal share of the gold at the Cattleman's. And the Governor's unconditional pardon goes with the loot."

A murmur rolled through the great company armed to its blackened teeth. Some of the shootists thought of saloons and every painted woman between Memphis and Frisco. Others thought of fertile farm land where a body could take root and grow along with his crops and children.

"Men, the rules be simple: Every man for hisself from here to the edge of town. But, Cedar City is off limits for gunplay. Do you all hear me on that? I'll make my stand at the edge of Main Street, by the liveries. . . . Him among you what crosses that line with your irons drawn will be dropped by me personal. There will be no shooting in town—except by me!"

The sheriff raised his shrill voice.

"Now boys, behind me is them hills. Yonder is the town—my town. When I leave here, you have until I get to town for to find your place and cover. But hear this: Not until I signal with my own rifle does this shoot get started. If I hear one round—just one—before I fire, the whole deal is off and I'll not be dealing with you again except to cut you down from a rope! Remember, the first shot is mine."

One hundred hands fell from their handirons to lay fitfully at their sides or upon saddle horns. The word of the Cedar City sheriff was just that good.

The sheriff slid down from his high rock. The throng reined their mounts to clear a path from the sheriff's rocky pulpit to his horse tied to a sapling wilted by the dry heat. The lawman walked quickly to his animal and mounted. At full gallop, his trail of dust shimmered along the road leading to Cedar City.

Before the sheriff was out of sight, the throng exploded in all directions. But not a weapon was cocked. A thick and choking cloud of dust rose toward the purple sky as four hundred hooves pounded the earth toward rocky hills, scrub brush cover, and small box canyons. Above the swirling dust, a chilling chorus of yelps and shouts drove terrified horses onward. The new sun could not penetrate the cloud of dry ground churning in the thin air.

Through the suffocating cloud, the four Hart Brothers and Doc spurred their mounts into the hills. Rounding a rocky cliff baked white by the desert sun, the five riders halted in a narrow ravine. Men and horses panted hard of the hot air. In minutes, the rocky wilderness absorbed all of the hard men leaving only the lingering cloud of dust behind.

For fifteen long minutes, men in every crook and crag watched the purple sky and their backs. Then a volley of rifle fire rolled lazily through the stifling heat. A heartbeat later, the thin air erupted with musketry. In the first moments of the Cedar City Rendezvous, a dozen men fell from their dusty saddles and dropped to the salty desert ground.

THE TIGHTLY SHUTTERED town was silent. Store fronts were boarded shut like Kansas awaiting black and grinding funnel clouds. Not a man nor beast braved the morning street as the distant thunder from the desert rolled into town. The far horizon was obscured by a rising cloud of dust and smoke. Only the Cedar City sheriff stood in the sunshine. He leaned against the livery at the end of Main Street. Over head, the great banner sagged limply, its black letters faded.

Leaning against a post, the town sheriff squinted into the distance. He put fire to his pipe and sent smoke rings toward the perfect sky. The dull report of musketry sounded far away in the dry air thinned by the morning heat. It will not take long, he thought.

Behind the sheriff, three blocks up the dirt boulevard, the white sun shone blindingly on the wavy glass windows of the Cattleman's. Inside the stone and iron fortress, anxious tellers huddled in corners. The tile floor and cold walls echoed the distant gunplay.

The tall cashier swallowed hard at the teller's window furthest from the front double doors.

"Morning, Mr. Thompson," the black-frocked Deacon said without smiling. Sweat followed the deep furrows in his wind-burned cheeks.

The Deacon was the only patron in the Cattleman's. The guards with rifles at the door looked like Prussians. Their gaze did not leave the Deacon's back.

"Guess it's time to make that little withdrawal, Mr. Thompson. Seems everyone else has picked a perfect day to blow themselves away."

"What will it be, sir," the teller croaked. His mouth was drier than the street outside.

"Perhaps we should step to the back." The Deacon's wide smile drained the last color from the cashier's face. The banker glanced at the guards at the front door. He looked pained.

The Deacon pulled his Prince Albert coat tighter around the heavy handirons at his hips. At the same instant, the attention of the guards out front was distracted by an awful crying from the street. The four armed men pushed through the doorway into the terrible sun.

"Oh Gawd! Oh Gawd!"

No Account writhed in spasms of agony on the front porch of the Cattleman's Bank and Trust. He rolled on his backside while he clutched at his chest. Over the bearded, little man, the four guards knelt and laid hands on the mountain man who cried pitifully. His profuse sweat smelled like strong soap. Spittle drooled from his gasping mouth. His hands were inside his leather tunic.

Inside the Cattleman's, cashiers peered through the iron bars of their cages to spy the terrible drama of life and death on their doorstep. Far behind them, the Deacon and the young teller looked at each other.

"The vault, Mr. Thompson. . . . Time is money."

At the far end of the dirt street, the Cedar City sheriff heard only the distant rumble of gunfire. He could not hear the death rattle of No Account by the side of the road.

ᒪ

"LOOK OUT!" BELLOWED Jason as he earred back the hammer of his aged Remington and blasted over the shoulder of Samuel. The handiron belched white sulphur behind a spinning roundball. The lead plowed into the breast of a mounted man whose animal stumbled and fell ten feet from the middle brother. The gunman fell to earth and coughed violet blood into the sand filling his mouth. His wide eyes did not see his horse lying nearby. The horse kicked furiously at the hot air. The noble beast's intestines had fatally twisted during his rolling fall and his death by strangulation of his bowels would be slow and agonizing.

The brothers' horses pranced beside the dead rider and his dying mount.

"Thanks," Samuel shouted over the thundering gunfire surrounding them.

"That way!" ordered the oldest brother. The five riders gathered their reins and charged from their ravine into the pulsating daylight.

Into the open space they rode hard for the barren hills bordering the road to town. Behind them and around them, the air whizzed with spinning bullets and shrieking horseflesh.

"There!" Luke shouted, leading the way into the rocky hills. They stopped with their horses skidding upon the fetlocks of their bloodied, hind legs. Dropping his reins, Jason reloaded his awkward, cap-and-ball revolver while his mount spun in tight circles between Doc and the other three brothers. All five animals carried their ears flat back and their eyes showed white with horse fear.

Before Jason could drop the empty cylinder and roll a loaded one into the revolver's frame, a lone rider flew over the crest of a small hill. The gunman stood in his stirrups and held his reins between his teeth. Both of his hands were filled with hot iron.

The white-eyed shootist and his mount were airborne over the little rise before the four brothers and Doc could clear leather. Biting his reins until his mouth bled, the rider swung both Peacemakers toward Doc whose animal spun wildly in a cloud of fine dust.

A single report from the stranger's piece sent a .44-40 ball over Jason's shoulder. Through the weapon's smoke, Frank fired pointblank into the assailant's throat. The youngest brother yelled mindlessly as he fired between the ear's of his wild mount.

Stranger and horse tumbled down the hill. The man fell face down beside his convulsing animal. But the rider's head was not quite connected to the massive wound in his neck. The back of the head came to rest on his spine. Blood squirted in rhythmic bursts from the ruptured neck. Quickly, the body was covered with fine, white dust rising from the stamping feet of the five horses of Doc and the brothers.

But the saddle on Doc's spinning mount was empty. Doc's horse bucked furiously and bounded off into the desert. The empty saddle's stirrups beat the animal's flanks and drove him on in blind panic.

NO ACCOUNT GRIPPED his sides inside his blouse beneath the four, kneeling guards.

"Thank ye kindly," No Account grinned with black teeth. Abruptly, he stopped his anguished squirming. When he pulled his hands from his buckskin tunic, each hand was heavy with a six-shooter. No Account steadied his weapons under the nostrils of the aghast faces of the guards crouched beside him. The guards rocked back on their heels but they did not rise from the two muzzles aimed at their faces.

Inside the Cattleman's, the Deacon smiled at the tall cashier.

"The vault, if you please," the man in black ordered calmly.

The other tellers craned their white necks toward the sidewalk. When No Account's cries stopped suddenly, each cashier lowered his eyes. Dead, they thought.

"Easy now, Mr. Thompson." The Deacon spoke softly toward the teller's back, which he followed behind the other cashiers' cages. None of the sweating bankers turned toward the passing Deacon and his escort as the pair walked slowly toward the rear of the bank. The Deacon rested both hands on the ivory handles of his irons still concealed in bulges under his waistcoat.

"Watch your step, Mr. Thompson," the Deacon said in a whisper sounding like gravel underfoot.

On each side of the vault door stood two guards toting Winchester repeating rifles and Colt Peacemakers in their belts.

"It's alright," the banker breathed with all of his energy.

"Morning, gents," the Deacon smiled warmly. He had crossed his arms on his black coat away from the twin bulges underneath.

Neither guard showed teeth when he stepped aside to permit the two men to enter the huge vault chamber hewn from stone blocks fit for a Pharaoh's tomb.

In the gloomy vault, Mr. Thompson's trembling hand lit an oil lamp. The Deacon reached into his deep pockets and pulled out two large pouches of thick leather. The two sacks were connected by a single strap. When the Deacon did not draw his weapons from his pockets, the wind rushed loudly from the banker's dry mouth.

"Fill 'em up, if you please, sir," the Deacon whispered under the flickering lamp. Each man breathed more deeply in the damp vault which felt like a cave. The lamp consumed oxygen like a third man and the narrow chamber closed in upon both men as the air became stale.

Mr. Thompson shook visibly at the iron wheel of the inner safe's door. He stared at it with wide eyes as if he were confronting the worst nightmare of childhood.

"But I don't know the combination . . . I swear to you!" The banker whispered hoarsely. He licked his salty lips.

"Best make one up, boy." The Deacon spoke through clenched teeth in low tones so close to the guards just outside. "And hurry."

The youth gulped and slowly twisted the numbered dial on the door. When he jerked the wheel, the door did not budge. He blinked burning sweat out of his eyes.

"Damn," the banker whimpered to himself. His fingers left smudges on the dial which glistened in the lamp light. His wide eyes followed the Deacon's free hand which glided to his gun belt. The cashier's white shirt was now clinging to his body. The safe dial spun again.

The Deacon's eyes opened wide when the iron door clanked open.

"The sheriff's word is good after all," the man in black sighed.

The teller did not turn around to face the armed stranger. He simply reached over for the Deacon's leather sacks. The banker filled each bag with smaller sacks of gold coins. When both pouches were full of gold, the Deacon handed them to Mr. Thompson who stumbled sideways under the load of fifty pounds of yellow metal. The teller blinked the sweat from his eyes so fast that he appeared to be crying silently.

The Deacon removed his waistcoat and folded it over his arm. Standing in the yellow light, the taller man took the twin sacks and slipped the thick strap behind his neck. The two sacks fell heavily to his sides, one behind each holster. Under the weight, the Deacon was stooped over as he panted and pulled the black coat over his black vest. The teller watched in dumb silence as the gunman adjusted his coat and the sacks of treasure underneath.

"Thanks much," the Deacon smiled. Open in front, the long coat concealed the strap and the gold hanging behind the two revolvers. "Let's go," the Deacon ordered softly. The banker gently closed the safe door and followed the highwayman out of the vault past the two grim guards.

"Fine day, ain't it?" the Deacon nodded to the armed men who retook their places on either side of the vault. Their faces did not twitch at the tall man's feigned courtesy.

"After you," the older man smiled to the banker.

The teller drenched in sweat led the Deacon through the back of the bank toward the cashiers' cages. The young man took his place behind the bars and the Deacon took his in front.

"Thank you for the hospitality. You did well, boy. And you were quite right." The big man smiled a grin that sent a shiver down the young man's spine. "You were right, Mr. Thompson. No one could take this fine bank from outside. And, if you want to live to have grand-children, I shall require a five-minute headstart."

When the youth tried to nod, he trembled so violently that he had to hold onto the little counter at his waist. The Deacon's face suddenly softened.

"Live long, Mr. Thompson." The tall man's hard face lost its cold glare and his words were almost warm. "One day, you will bounce your grandchildren on your knee and tell them about today. When you do . . . tell them that you did business with The Deacon." He bowed slightly and turned away.

The teller was completely paralyzed. He could not have called for the guards even if the Deacon had ordered it.

Into the blinding daylight and the wilting heat, the Deacon stumbled under the weight inside his coat. He stopped on the wooden sidewalk where he towered over the four guards immobilized by the two hand-irons aimed up at them by No Account who still laid spread-eagle on the hot porch.

"Now boys," the Deacon spoke slowly to the four men who dared not rise. His words came out like a school master's. "You can either stop an arsenal of lead right here and now, or you can get up real easy and truck on over to the nearest saloon and tip one on me."

The big man laid his hands on each ivory-handled weapon on his aching hips.

"Well?"

On the ground, No Account smiled a black and mindless grin into the four gray faces. Wide-open pores on each guard's face leaked onto his bent knees.

"A drink sounds just fine in this here heat," one of the men stammered. He swallowed hard.

"Sounds reasonable," the Deacon smiled.

The four men decked out like Mexican colonels rose slowly. The Deacon put his face close to the one who had spoken: a face with sunken eyes and the blank expression of a man who dreams only of things he can smell. The gunman laid four gold coins into the palm. To the Deacon, the man's hand felt like the belly of a fish.

"Well, go on," the Deacon ordered. The four men ran off on stiff legs, which made them appear to hop toward the first saloon on Main Street. Each loping runner scrunched up his back and lowered his head to make a smaller target.

No Account scooted on his backside out of the doorway of the bank. Not until he was well clear of the open door and the eyes inside the bank did he stand. He returned his two handirons to his leathers.

"I done good," the bearded little man grinned.

The Deacon flared his nostrils at the aroma simmering on No Account.

"The best," the Deacon nodded.

"Trouble inside?"

"No. Now let's burn some daylight before the teller finds his tongue." The Deacon looked anxiously up the dirt street. He raised his hands to balance the great weight at his sides which sent jabs of pain down his back.

No Account chuckled childishly and stepped into the fierce sunshine of the street. The Deacon followed him off the sidewalk. Fifty pounds of gold coin bent the tall man's broad back.

When the Deacon stepped down from the landing, he laid his right boot into a fresh splat of tobacco spittle which hit the dusty ground together with the gunman's spurs.

"DOC!" FRANK CRIED out, diving from his foaming horse. He landed on his knees beside the dead but twitching corpse of the freshly dispatched stranger. Next to this decapitated meat, Doc lay sprawled on the white sand. He was face-down in the tracks made by his fleeing horse.

"Mount up, damn you!" Luke yelled from atop his animal still spinning out of control.

"There ain't time!" Jason shouted.

"Doc!" the youth repeated above the roar of screaming killers and whining lead balls. He rolled the old man face-up under the blinding, white sun. "Gawd," the brother breathed.

Doc's arms were limp at his sides. In the center of his shirt, blood spurted out in a pulsating fountain a full six inches into the dry air. The youth knew only to ram his filthy finger deep into the neat hole to dam the surging leak of the old man's red life.

"Doc?" the youngest brother pleaded, choking on the dust storm rising from the feet of the horses spinning behind him. Samuel held the reins of Frank's mount which lay back on its hind legs and struggled wildly to escape the smoky fury and gunfire.

The old man opened one dim eye. He squinted against the fierce sun directly overhead. With his free hand, the youth shaded Doc's eyes from the painful glare. Blood gurgled from the wounded man's throat and trickled from his mouth and nostrils. Deep inside Doc's chest, the youth's hot finger felt the contractions of the old heart which quivered slightly between each weakening thump.

"You cain't stay here, boys," Doc whispered, licking blood from his cracked lips. When Doc was seized by bloody coughs, Frank felt his finger rub against Doc's breastbone.

"For the love of God, boy!" Jason shouted.

"Thank Gawd," Doc sighed. His eyes were closed in the shade of Frank's raised hand. "Thank Gawd I have sons now to put me under Christianlike." Doc inhaled and his chest rose so high that the youth's finger half emerged from the warm hole. The gasping breast fell, the old lungs filled with foam, and the blue lips parted. Doc's stubbled chin pointed toward the awful sun. His chest rose no more.

The youngest brother with the new hat and with tears making rivulets on his muddy face rocked back on his heels. He knelt beside two warm corpses. When he pulled his finger from the old man's torn heart, blood and watery serum oozed from the hole in the quiet chest.

"Now, brother!" Jason screamed. "We'll come back! . . . My word on it!" For an instant, the oldest brother's horse stood still. "Now mount up before we join the old man."

As the youth rose on shaking legs, he wiped the sticky blood from his hands onto his dusty shirt. Two mounted men suddenly took the crest of the little hill behind the brothers. The riders with irons drawn pounded down upon the four brothers.

"Sweet Jesus!" Luke shouted as his animal spun between his aching legs. At his outburst, Jason and Samuel opened fire on the approaching riders who caught a wall of lead in their faces.

Doc and his killer laid side by side. Onto their bodies, the two attacking riders tumbled in a cloud of dust. The youngest brother skipped aside as one man landed limply across Doc's wide-eyed face. The other rider dropped heavily on the legs of Doc's killer. Four dead men now reposed at the feet of the four brothers.

The cadaver across Doc's face lay twitching face-down. The back of his head was gone. Between Frank's feet the second gunman lay on his back. His whole hand was impaled within a massive wound in his side. Only his bloodied wrist was visible outside. Blood and dark bile flowed down his arm. His mouth opened and closed slowly, like a fish thrown onto dry land.

When Samuel handed the leathers to Frank, he heaved himself into the saddle.

Through the swirling dust, the brothers followed their own tracks along the base of a hill toward the road. In the noontime daylight, their horses leaped over the pile of bodies. The scene along the road was a battlefield, the morning after.

The brothers galloped headlong into a dozen men riding hard for town. Some rode with their reins in their teeth. Some rode with one hand pushing their bowels back into their bellies while their free hands fired hot revolvers.

Jason rode with Frank on his left and Luke and Samuel on his right. They all fired blind into the surrounding rabble.

With a throaty cry such as the brothers had last heard from the closed room where Frank was being birthed, Jason reeled in his saddle. He dropped his Remington into the churning sea of dust and gripped his saddle horn. He leaned full forward onto his animal's neck and his right hand clutched his side where a red splash gathered dust quickly.

"DOING A LITTLE business so early?" the sweating marshal said. He emerged from behind a horse tied to a hitching rail at the Deacon's side. On the Deacon's far side, No Account stood open-mouthed with his hands inching toward his open tunic.

"Not a good idea," the marshal growled toward No Account.

The Deacon stood like a black statue in the deserted street under a purple sky. Slowly, the tall man crossed his arms over his black coat. His white shirt gleamed in the sunshine.

In the distance, the crack of gunfire grew steadily louder and closer. But the volleys were fewer and the silence between shots, longer. A burst of fire from the desert rumbled past the town sheriff four blocks away and over the three men facing off in the bright street.

In the blink of an eye, No Account pulled his iron from his shirt.

Before the grubby little man at the Deacon's side could ear back the hammer, the marshal cleared leather and cocked his revolver before it was waist high.

The marshal's shot shattered No Account's breast-bone before he could get a round off. No Account tumbled backward, bowled over by the lead ball which exploded his pounding heart. Airborne, No Account dropped his weapon as he spun face-down toward the street. He flopped into a dark puddle of his own blood and bone fragments which had beaten him to the ground. No Account stopped breathing before he hit the sandy street.

The marshal turned his hot iron to the Deacon who remained motionless with his arms still crossed. The retired lawman held his fire and spat a ribbon of chew toward the Deacon's feet. The projectile raised a tiny cloud of dust between the Deacon's boots.

When the marshal lowered his handiron, he and the Deacon looked into each other's eyes. There was no shadow between them with the white sun overhead. In the distance, only a few bursts of gunfire rolled up the street.

"Your move, Marshal," the Deacon said softly. He squinted toward the mirrorlike windows behind the lawman. The gold lettering glared in the sunshine "Cattleman's Bank and Trust."

With the fluid grace of a well-oiled machine, the marshal jerked up his iron and cocked the black hammer. The Deacon's hands were only hip high when the marshal's iron exploded.

When the spinning ball pierced the Deacon's long coat belt-high, the impact knocked him backwards. He went down hard on one black knee while he cocked both of his weapons which he drew as he fell.

Each of the Deacon's pieces erupted into a single, white clap of thunder in the marshal's face.

On the marshal's shirt stained with tobacco juice was the dark outline of a five-pointed star near the large man's heart.

Beside the star shape, a red gouge burst open with a splash of blood where two lead balls roared into the same hole. The marshal stumbled, dropped his handiron, and fell sideways. Dust rose where he landed on his back. His red hands pressed a whistling wound in his chest. Lungshot, the big man's breast rattled with escaping air and frothy liquid. He lay quietly with his face contorted and his back arched. He supported his body only with the back of his bare head and his spurred heels.

The Deacon stood, coughing and pale. He lowered his irons to his dusty sides. Above the dying lawman, the Deacon opened his coat. The black cloth fell behind the empty holsters and revealed two heavy sacks hanging at the big man's hips. One of the leather bags bore a dark hole where the marshal's single bullet had entered. Inside the satchel, the soft lead shot had vaporized against a bag of gold coins. The Deacon caught his breath and stooped to pick up his black hat.

"Morning to you, Marshal," the Deacon smiled coldly as he aimed his revolver at the downed man's forehead. He stepped over No Account and turned so he faced the empty street.

A single ball spun loudly from the Deacon's iron. The soft lead plowed sloppily into the marshal's sweating brow, through the gelatinous repository of half a century of memories, and on through the fallen man's skull into the ground. The shattered head jerked when a surge of gray meat foamed out of the ears.

The marshal's hands soaked with pink blood dropped limply to his sides. The air stopped bubbling from his lungs. The star shaped patch was lost in a red pool.

From the corner of a barred window in the deserted jail, a thin girl with short hair and a hard face blinked wide, violet eyes. Then she turned and vanished into the shadows.

With the bank behind him, the Deacon stood with his black legs straddling the marshal's body. He returned his warm irons to his hips.

When the world behind the Deacon exploded in a searing flash, he took a single step forward. Very calmly, he lowered his face toward his chest. He saw the dead marshal's face and shirt covered with pink splatter. The Deacon's lungs trickled down the marshal's body.

The Deacon's numb legs melted into the thin air and he felt himself floating painlessly downward toward the dead man's body.

The Deacon opened his arms as if to embrace the marshal upon whom he bounced and rolled off onto his back.

Close to No Account laying face-down, the marshal and the Deacon laid side by side, silently staring into the blinding sun and into the smoking barrels of the shotgun held by Mr. Thompson. The banker trembled and wept on the wooden sidewalk in front of his stone fortress.

Chapter Seventeen

"EASY, BROTHER," THE SMALL MAN urged as he pushed back the struggling shoulders of the figure beneath starched sheets. The bedridden man lay back. Sweat soaked his bearded face.

Jason panted with Samuel resting his full weight upon the supine man's arms. The stricken man's hair was matted on the pillow.

Throbbing pain gripped the side of the man moaning in bed. Under the covers, his hand sought the deep torment which burned hotly. He found a thick bandage wrapped tightly around his middle. He took frequent and shallow breaths against the constraining wraps.

"Steady now, brother," Samuel said, releasing his grip on Jason's feverish body.

Jason opened his eyes. Through a hazy film, he focussed in the sooty light from an oil lamp near his bed. His fogged vision took in familiar surroundings at the Grand Hotel.

Jason sucked in his breath. He grimaced at the pain shooting down his legs. He shivered painfully from fever and shock. His limbs were far away from his mind, but they had left the pain behind.

"How long?" the oldest brother whispered through his stupor.

"Two days. Going on three. It's about midnight now. The doctor said you have to rest." Samuel smoothed the white sheet over his brother's chest. Perspiration was soaking through to the top sheet. Samuel dropped back into his chair beside the bed. Both men were exhausted.

Jason mustered all of his strength to open his eyes. He surveyed the room for familiar faces. He saw only his middle brother. When he became aware of the two missing brothers, he thrashed again at his sheets.

"Our brothers!" the wounded man begged.

Samuel rose to restrain Jason.

"Easy, now. Easy. Frank and Luke are fine. . . . Believe me."

The patient closed his eyes. He labored to whip his hazy brain back from the pain. It took many minutes of concentration to remember the terrible, bloodied desert. Samuel thought the delirious man slept in the moment of silence.

"I remember now," Jason sighed without opening his wet eyes. "Our brothers are safe?"

"Well and fit. They're at the livery brushing out the animals. Got back an hour ago."

"Back?"

"Yes. Had to go back out into the desert before night-fall. Old Doc, you know. They had to go back to plant old Doc decent. Promised."

"Doc. Yes," Jason mumbled. "And that marshal, and the Deacon, and that squirrelly fellow, No Account?"

"All dead, right outside there." Samuel did not tax his brother with the details.

Jason nodded his aching head. Slowly, his mind came back to the reason for his pain and for all of the sudden death.

"The gold?" the oldest brother inquired as he stroked his side.

"Have to buy a mule to carry our share home." The middle brother grinned. "Maybe two mules."

Like big city medicine, the words revived the groggy patient.

"It was all true then? The sheriff's word was good?"

"True as our fortune tucked away at the Cattleman's across the street. Signed, sealed, and just waiting for you to mend and be back on your feed again."

"Feed?" Jason smiled limply. "Last thing on my mind right now is food." He chuckled until the pain in his searing bowels made him stop. "Feels like you'll need a third mule to haul me."

"We can afford one now. But you'll come around in a day or two. It's just the laudanum what's got you laid up. Town doc says you'll be a might turned around by it for another few days. But it's good for the pain."

In the warm and sooty glow from the lamp, Jason closed his eyes.

"Yep," Samuel said softly. "Doc had to dig pretty deep to fetch out the lead in your gut. But he says he left all of your plumbing behind. Said you'll always know a day in advance when rain's coming." Samuel smiled.

As a weak smile cracked across the hurting man's face, the door opened. Luke and Frank entered the little room. Their boots left dusty prints on the carpet. They carried their hats caked with trail.

"How's he doing, Samuel?" Frank whispered. His voice was full of fatigue from burying his friend: a promise kept.

"No need to tip-toe," the patient sighed without opening his drugged eyes.

"Well," Luke smiled as he stroked his red beard. He touched the corner of his glistening eye.

"Strong as an ox," Frank smiled widely. "I'll be damned."

"Mind your mouth, boy," the oldest brother ordered weakly. Perspiration ran down his white cheeks.

"Yes, mother," the youngest brother smiled.

"What about that girl—the whore?"

"Gone," Frank shrugged. "Rode out alone right after the shoot. Bought the dead marshal's horse. Dressed up like a boy again. No guns. No water. Just done rode off north, into the desert. The smithy told me. Must be shrivelled to nothing by now." Frank shook his head. "She sure had pretty eyes."

"Samuel says the sheriff's word is good?" Jason asked as he fought sleep.

"Sterling." Luke swatted his knee with his dirty hat. A cloud of dust filled the room and Jason coughed deeply. "Doc says you can ride by week's end."

Jason was losing his fight with drugged sleep. He could only nod and part his lips. A bead of perspiration trickled off the end of his sun burned nose.

"And then," Frank began beside Samuel who had kept the nighttime vigil.

"And then home . . . all four of us," Luke sniffed. He wiped his nose with the back of his dirty hand.

Jason did not speak. Sleep alighted mercifully upon his tortured chest. Slowly, his pain drifted away. The oil lamp illuminated the faint smile of one homeward bound with his brothers by blood and his brothers of the trail where a man is only as safe as his companions are brave and true.